CW00524297

A HOME FOR THE ALIEN WARRIOR

TREASURED BY THE ALIEN

HONEY PHILLIPS

BEX MCLYNN

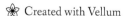 Created with Vellum

CHAPTER ONE

C laire heard the door to the underground lab open, accompanied by the sound of voices, and her heart started to thud uncomfortably against her ribs. The twins heard the door as well and stiffened, their small bodies going rigid. The smiles she had managed to coax out of them disappeared, and her heart ached as they quickly stuffed the small cards they had been using to play a game into the storage locker. They were so young to have been forced to learn such discipline.

"But I don't want her," she heard Dr. Pagalan, the scientist in charge of the laboratory, protest. "I want an older female."

"I know, Scholar Pagalan," the other voice said smoothly, and Claire recognized it. Kwan, the alien bastard who had stolen her from Earth and sold her to Pagalan for his experiments. "This is simply temporary," he continued. "I have another buyer lined up for her, but he couldn't be here in time for the sale."

"That's not my problem."

"I know, but unfortunately, there are rumors that the Patrol is interested in our activities. We had to close down the main auction site, and I need a place for her to stay."

"Why me? I'm a very busy male."

"I understand, but you're the only one I trust to, err, return her in the same condition. You may not value her virginity, but her buyer is quite insistent that it remain intact."

Claire shivered as the twins crept closer, curling against her on either side. As far as she could tell, despite his interest in reproduction, Pagalan had no interest at all in the actual act of sex. A lack for which she had given thanks many times.

"I don't know," Pagalan muttered. "I dislike having my routine disturbed."

"She won't be any trouble. Will you, girl?"

A soft cry followed Kwan's words, and Claire clenched her fists. *That bastard.*

"And if you do me this favor, I promise that I will provide you with your preferred type of female on my next trip. At a discount."

That was sure to appeal to the scientist. He was extremely tight-fisted.

"Very well," Dr. Pagalan said begrudgingly as the inner door to their room opened. "In here, girl. The older female will tell you what is expected."

A young alien female was pushed through the open door. She had soft golden fur and definite feline characteristics, but despite the strange features, Claire could see that she was extremely pretty. The girl immediately put her back to the wall, managing to look scared and defiant at the same time.

The two males remained in the doorway, Kwan looking speculatively from the twins to her.

"Do you think you were successful this time?"

"I believe so. I should know shortly."

Claire resisted the impulse to put her hand to her stomach.

Dr. Pagalan's words filled her with an agonizing mixture of hope and dread. How ironic that this alien scientist could be the one to give her what she longed for most but would also—if he was successful—be the one to take it away from her.

"If you can consistently produce twins, it would be most profitable," Kwan added.

"I'm not interested in profit. I am interested in the advance of knowledge. I have already prepared a paper..." Pagalan's eyes burned with fanatical zeal, and Claire breathed a sigh of relief as he guided Kwan back into the corridor and locked the door again.

The new girl looked around the sterile room, and Claire followed her gaze. A wide padded shelf for sleeping ran along one wall, while a small storage cabinet and the door to the bathroom occupied the opposite wall. A work table and four hard chairs comprised the only other furnishings. As usual everything was spotlessly clean. Even though Dr. Pagalan showed no inclination towards tidiness himself, he insisted that their room be kept neat at all times. She suspected it was a matter of control rather than any real desire for tidiness, but they had all learned to obey.

"What is this place?"

A cage. Claire bit back her first response and tried to come up with a more neutral answer.

"This is Dr. Pagalan's lab." She pointed to the wide observation panel next to the door. The scientist's workroom was clearly visible through a matching window on the other side of the corridor.

"Don't worry," she added quickly when the girl flinched. "You're not here for his experiments."

"But you are?" The girl frowned at her. "You are human?"

"Yes. How did you know? You've met other humans?"

She had always suspected that there must be others, even

though she'd never seen anyone else. It had never seemed logical that the aliens would have come all the way to Earth just for her.

The night she had been taken, she'd been having a restless night haunted by memories, and around midnight, that restlessness had finally driven her from her small home and workshop. It had never even occurred to her that she might be in danger. Although Crystal Lake was close enough to the boutiques in the larger ski towns for her to sell the crafts she made to occupy her time, it was too small to attract many tourists. As she walked past the tiny business district and down the hill to the lake that gave the town its name, all she had been thinking about was the past.

But as she stood looking at the stars and the path the moon made across the water, she'd felt a sudden, sharp pain in her neck, and then the world went dark. She had regained consciousness in a sterile white room—a hospital, her panicked mind immediately assumed—but her body wouldn't respond.

"Why an older female?" A male voice spoke from somewhere to her left, but she couldn't turn her head to see who was speaking.

"Dr. Pagalan specifically requested one. One of his considerations is trying to extend the fertile years."

"Foolishness." The first voice sounded disgruntled. "Young breeders and infants. They are the most profitable."

"And the most difficult to obtain without arousing attention." She could almost hear the shrug in the other man's voice. "As long as there is profit to be made, I don't care. And Pagalan is still willing to spend his inheritance on his project."

"It won't last much longer at this rate." The man snorted. "You do realize he's insane, don't you, Kwan?"

"Quite possibly. Although if he does succeed, it opens up a whole new revenue stream."

She tried to open her mouth, to protest, but all that came out was a faint, garbled noise. Apparently, it was enough to interrupt the conversation. A face swam into view above her. A not human face. Matte black hair topped a face with plastic-looking white skin and eyes that had a distinct reddish glow. *Alien,* her horrified mind screamed. He regarded her with no more interest than she would have given to an insect.

"She's coming out of it. Put her back under while I finish processing her."

And the world went dark again.

When she woke a second time, she was in a small white cell. The white-faced aliens—Vedeckians, she had learned—fed her regularly but otherwise ignored her, refusing to answer any questions. She estimated about three weeks had passed before one of them entered her cell and placed a silver collar around her neck, paying no attention to her protests. It wasn't until he marched her out of the cell and down a landing ramp that she realized the collar was more than symbolic.

When they reached the bottom of the ramp and she saw what was unmistakably a city surrounding them, she tried to make a break for it. She didn't have a plan, didn't know where she was going, but she was convinced it had to be better than whatever they had in mind for her. He let her get three steps away before raising a small device. A bolt of searing agony sizzled through her veins, sending her to knees.

The bastard laughed, then picked her up with a casual strength that belied his slender build and threw her over his shoulder. He dumped her unceremoniously in the back of an odd-looking vehicle and brought her here to Dr. Pagalan's house of horrors.

The scientist had met them at the door of what looked like some decaying Gothic mansion, his disheveled orange hair in a wild halo around his scaly white face like some alien Einstein. He looked her over, mouth pursed.

"Is that the best you have to offer me, Kwan?"

"You wanted an older female."

"I suppose she'll have to do." He started to reach for her arm, but the Vedeckian snatched her back.

"Credits first."

"Fine, fine. But you owe me a discount after that last debacle."

The two of them had haggled over her price while she stood there seething with rage—and fear. Only the lingering weakness from the shock and the painful sparks still traveling through her nervous system kept her from trying to run again. And then the two males had reached an agreement and it was too late.

She shuddered, and Juni put a small hand on her knee, bringing her back to the present. Enormous dark eyes, a striking contrast to the child's pale blue skin and silky pink hair, gave her a worried look. Claire sighed and hugged the girl. Juni never spoke, but she had an uncanny way of knowing when someone else was upset.

"I'm fine, sweetie." She looked back over at the new female and forced a smile. "Yes, I'm human. My name is Claire."

"I'm Neera. I recognized you because my mother's cousin is mated to a human. Although she is not very much like you. Her skin is darker, and she is very... elegant."

Neera's glance was faintly disparaging, and Claire did her best not to flinch. The girl was wearing a soft tunic and matching loose pants in a pale shade of green and, despite whatever she had been through, had the well-kept look of someone who took care of herself. At one time, Claire had taken a similar pride in her appearance, but she had abandoned regular haircuts and manicures when she abandoned corporate life. She had been abducted wearing jeans, flip-flops, and an old sweatshirt. Dr. Pagalan had found the clothes cumbersome and summarily replaced them with a garment that resembled a shapeless hospital gown, although at least it sealed up the front. He'd graciously let her keep the flip-flops.

"Our captor hasn't given me any time to go shopping," she said dryly.

"Alicia would still look elegant," the girl said definitely, then winced. "I'm sorry. I know it's foolish to assume that every member of a race will be the same. I learned that lesson."

The last words were accompanied by a bitterness that looked wrong on such a young face.

"What happened?" she asked softly.

"I made a mistake. I thought I was in love, but it turned out the only thing he was in love with was making a profit." Neera sighed, then crossed the room and sat down next to her. "I'm a fool."

"Love can be tricky." She knew that all too well herself.

"Yeah. I'm never going to hear the end of it when my cousin Rafalo finds me."

"Your cousin?"

"Yes, he's the one mated to the human. He's always been protective—overprotective, I would have said before—and I'm sure he's looking for me."

Claire hesitated, not sure how to respond. She didn't want to destroy the girl's hopes, but was it realistic to expect that the male would find her?

"I know what you're thinking. But even though my mom likes to pretend it's not true, he has a lot of... connections that aren't exactly legal. If anyone can find me, he can." Neera looked down at her hands. "I just hope he isn't too late."

Claire covered the girl's hand with her own. "You just have to survive until he does."

"I'll try." Neera briefly returned her clasp, then looked over at the twins, peeping out from behind Claire. "And who are these two little charmers?"

"This is Beni and his sister, Juni. They know everything about this place. Isn't that right?"

Beni nodded, staring at Neera. "You're pretty."

"Thanks, squirt. You're pretty handsome yourself."

His little chest puffed out. "Do you wanna play a game?"

"Sure."

He dashed off to retrieve his precious pack of "cards." The cards were small pieces of paper that Claire had used to draw sets of mostly matching images. Lately, they had been using them to play a version of Go Fish, and Neera caught on quickly. Juni snuggled against Claire's side, watching them.

"Is everything all right, sweetheart?" Claire asked softly.

Juni tilted her head, the silky pink strands of her hair brushing against Claire's arm, then nodded firmly. Despite her youth, the girl was uncannily perceptive about people and if she approved of Neera, Claire trusted her judgment.

A short while later, Osata—one of the lab assistants—brought the evening meal, and they fell into the usual nighttime routine. The lab complex was never truly dark, but Claire had done her best to create some semblance of a normal life for the twins. After dinner and baths, she told them a story as they curled up together and drifted off to sleep.

"Where did the twins come from?" Neera asked softly once they had fallen asleep.

Claire sighed. "I can't be sure, but I think their mother was one of Dr. Pagalan's subjects."

She still remembered her horror when he had thrust her into this room and she had seen the two small children. They had been so quiet, so unchildlike, surveying her from those huge dark eyes. But then Juni had walked over and put her tiny hand in Claire's and Beni had given her a tentative smile. She had loved them ever since.

"What happened to her?"

"I'm not sure. They never talk about her, but Beni used to have nightmares. I think she died here."

"And he just kept them, locked away like this?"

"Yes. I sometimes think it's a miracle they survived. I'm not sure they would have if he had been solely responsible for their care, but he had another assistant when I arrived. I think Sarat did his best to look out for them."

She wouldn't have gone as far as calling Sarat a nice person—he did work for Dr. Pagalan after all—but he was kind to the twins. He always stopped to speak to them when he brought their meals, and he was the one responsible for the few toys they had. He had been kind to her as well, willing to answer her questions and tell her more about the world in which she found herself. But his interest in her had not been as platonic as his concern for the twins. Dr. Pagalan had caught him trying to kiss her one day and exploded in outrage. Muttering complaints about Sarat contaminating his experiments, he had immediately dismissed the male. Osata had been his replacement—silent, efficient, and completely uninterested in either the twins or Claire.

"This is no place for a child." Neera frowned at the sleeping children, then gave Claire a tremulous smile. "Or us. If he does find me, I'm sure my cousin won't leave any of you here."

The sudden, wild flare of hope was almost painful. She was always on the lookout for a way to escape—even going as far as to consider encouraging Sarat's interest in her in the hope that he would help them—but this was the closest she had come to a possibility.

That hope made it all the more agonizing when Dr. Pagalan unlocked the door a short time later.

"Come with me," he ordered.

As much as she hated it, she obeyed. The shock collar had taught her obedience. It didn't stop her from giving him a death glare as he led her into an exam room and strapped her down the table. The familiarity of the procedure didn't make it any more pleasant. He ran the scanner over her body, muttering at the findings, then inserted a long, thin needle into her abdomen. It was uncomfortable rather than painful, but every time he did it, she felt violated.

When he scowled at her, her heart sank. Even under the circumstances, she had hoped for a different result.

"It didn't work?"

"No. Useless female."

She refused to give him the satisfaction of a response as he led her back to their room. Neera was already asleep, and Claire climbed in behind the twins. The sense of loss haunted her, and the possibility of Neera's cousin coming to rescue them seemed like nothing more than an impossible dream. She cried herself silently to sleep.

CHAPTER TWO

Arcosta Nar'Taharan entered his quarters, closed the door behind him, and sighed. The small room on one of the lower levels of the busy space station was as neat and efficient as ever, the modest furnishings tucked away in the walls, but there was nothing welcoming or homelike about the place.

It's only temporary, he reminded himself as he stripped off his grease-stained overalls and headed for the minuscule sanitary facility. Determined to build up his savings as quickly as possible, he had deliberately chosen the least expensive private residence option available. He hadn't even indulged in the luxury of actual water. As the cleansing fluid poured down over his head, he focused on scrubbing away the grime of a long day spent working on a ship that should probably have been sent to the scrapheap a decade ago. But he had managed to get it running again, and he took no small satisfaction from that fact.

After he was clean, he yanked on a pair of training shorts, but before heading off to a practice room for some exercise, he pulled out his tablet and checked his notifications.

Mechanic shop for sale.

His heart started to beat a little faster, but he told himself not to be too optimistic. Most of the listings he found were unsuitable for one reason or another. But as he read on, his excitement continued to grow.

The shop, along with what was euphemistically called a rustic cabin and a large plot of ground, was located on Sampana. Sampana was one of the few planets that had not been devastated by the Red Death, the plague that had swept through the systems that made up the Confederated Planets more than twenty years ago, leaving nothing but death in its wake. The most heavily hit planets had large sections of abandoned and overgrown cities where people used to live. His own home planet, Ciresia, was one of them.

When he finally decided that he was tired of living a nomadic life, moving from ship to space station to another ship, he had considered returning to Ciresia. A quick survey had been enough to dissuade him. Even though the Council was trying to reestablish their society, the desolate conditions were a painful reminder of the civilization that had once flourished there. But Sampana had been sparsely populated to begin with, and its native population had been relatively unaffected. Also unlike Ciresia.

The plague had taken the future from the Cire race—it had taken all of their females. The knowledge that he would never find a mate and have a family of his own had kept him moving ever since he originally left the planet, but over the last few years he had come to realize that even without a mate, he wanted a home. He wanted to be able to walk out onto land that he owned and see the sky during the day and the stars at night. He wanted a house which belonged to him.

Or even a rustic cabin, he thought dryly, pushing away the thoughts of the past. The somewhat hazy images which accompanied the listing couldn't completely disguise the rundown nature of the building, but that didn't matter. With time, he could repair anything. And unlike the house, the shop appeared to be in good shape. Located on the edge of a small town, there should be enough local business to keep him occupied.

He flipped to the end of the listing to look at the price. *Fuck.* He was close, but it would take another six months of building up his savings to have the full purchase price. What were the odds that the property would still be available to him in six months? He wasn't the only one looking for a refuge, for a change in life.

Putting the tablet down with a regretful sigh, he pulled on a loose robe over his shorts and went off to the closest training room. But as he went through a series of basic exercises, then two less than challenging matches, thoughts of the property continued to haunt him.

"What a pitiful sight. A Cire warrior reduced to fighting children."

The mocking voice greeted him after the second match, and he looked up to find his friend Tangari grinning at him. The two of them had worked together several times over the years, before the Kissat male had finally acquired a ship of his own.

"Ignore him," Arcosta said to his young opponent. "Captain Tangari prefers to watch and criticize, not ruffle his own precious fur."

"I'm a lover, not a fighter." Tangari tossed his elaborately curled mane haughtily as the youngster grinned shyly and left them.

Despite his teasing, Arcosta knew the other male was actually an extremely deadly fighter and would be a much more challenging opponent. He eyed him speculatively.

"How about a match anyway? For old times sake."

Tangari gave an exaggerated shudder. "I'm flying out tomorrow, and I'd rather not spend the trip nursing my bruises."

"So soon?"

"I'm transporting balena oil. It pays well, but there's a lot of competition. I can't miss a delivery. But I'm here for the night and I've discovered a bar on the twentieth level where they brew their own paranat ale. Come with me and I'll buy you a drink."

Arcosta grinned, even as he shook his head. Tangari had always been able to find an exceptional place to drink anywhere they went.

"I should not."

"Why not? I remember when you were as eager as anyone for a drink at the end of a long day."

"I think you were always the most eager," he said dryly, and Tangari shrugged.

"I can't argue with you. But you've turned into a hermit since you started this quest of yours."

"I just decided that was more important to me."

"More important than your friends?"

Even though Tangari spoke lightly, Arcosta thought he detected a note of genuine hurt in his friend's voice. The thought of another evening in his bare cabin did not appeal to him.

"You are right. It has been a long time since we have had a chance to talk."

Tangari grinned and slapped him on the shoulder, then hustled him off to his latest discovery. As promised, the ale was exceptional, and two pitchers later, Arcosta found himself confiding in his friend about the property he'd discovered.

"I can't say I see the attraction in a shop on a backwater

planet," Tangari said thoughtfully. "But if that's what you want, why not go for it?"

"I told you. I do not have the credits for the purchase price."

"So finance it."

"In case it has escaped your notice, only the inner system planets have restored their banking infrastructure."

"What about a loan? I don't have the credits, or I would do it."

"You know what most of the moneylenders are like. Once you get in their clutches, it is hard to get out."

Tangari shuddered. "Yeah. I remember. Don't you know anyone rich?"

They both laughed, before they were interrupted by a pleasure companion.

"Looking for some company, gentlemales?"

"No, thank you," he said courteously, but he was a little surprised when Tangari also shook his head.

"Are you sure?" The female trailed her fingers teasingly down his arm.

For a moment, he was almost tempted, but he had learned long ago that any such encounter would ultimately be unsatisfying. A Cire male was wired to truly respond only to his mate.

"I thank you for the offer," he said sincerely. "But I do not indulge."

Tangari shot him a glance from across the table, but didn't say anything. When Arcosta rose to his feet, the other male followed.

"There is no need for you to cut your evening short," Arcosta told him.

Tangari shrugged. "As I said, I'm flying out tomorrow. I need to make sure that everything is ready."

He apologized gallantly to the female and ordered her a

pitcher of ale, then followed Arcosta out of the bar. At this hour of the evening, the corridors were still filled with crews from the various ships, as well as members of the station's personnel. Rather than attempting any further conversation, Tangari followed Arcosta silently back to his quarters.

"By the gods, you're living like a monk." Tangari shook his head, then shot Arcosta a look from under his brows. "Is it worth it?"

"It will be," he said with as much certainty as possible. "Do you never want to settle down?"

"Not usually. I was born in space, and I'll probably die in space. I'm too restless to be planet bound for long, although I was tempted once."

"Really?"

"There was a female." Tangari shrugged. "It did not end well."

Arcosta did his best to hide his surprise. Tangari was the last person he would have suspected of being serious enough about a female to consider giving up his ship. Before he could ask any questions, Tangari changed the subject.

"I was thinking about your problem," he said thoughtfully. "What about Rafalo?"

Rafalo owned the space station, and since Arcosta worked in one of the service facilities, he was technically his boss, although he had never met him personally.

"What about him?"

"Why not ask him for a loan? He's got more credits than any bank, and he's got a reputation for honest dealing."

"Honest?"

Tangari grinned and shrugged. "Perhaps honest is not exactly the correct word. But if he makes a deal, he will honor it."

Arcosta considered the matter. Tangari was correct. And

although the station owner's previous reputation gave him pause, Rafalo dealt fairly with his workers and did limit what was allowed on the station.

"Why would he give me a loan? He does not know me."

Tangari gave him a shrewd look. "He knows everything that goes on at the station. It wouldn't surprise me that he knows who you are. Plus, you are a Cire."

"Why does that matter?"

"Because it means he can trust you to repay the debt. You wouldn't run out on him, would you?"

"Of course not," he growled, offended by the suggestion.

"You see?"

When Arcosta didn't reply, Tangari changed the subject again. They swapped stories for another hour before he left, promising to be back in a few months.

As Arcosta prepared for bed, he found himself replaying the other male's words. Was Tangari right? Would Rafalo give him a loan? As much as he disliked the idea of being indebted to anyone, he also didn't want to miss this opportunity.

The next morning, after a restless night, he stopped by the station's main office to make an appointment. Instead, he was immediately ushered into Rafalo's office. The Kissat male was beginning to show his age, threads of white in his mane and around his mouth, but he moved with the ease of a much younger male and his eyes were exceptionally penetrating.

"Ah, Arcosta. How fortunate. I was about to send for you."

He wasn't exactly surprised that Rafalo knew his name—he suspected that the male kept close watch on the station's business—but he was surprised that he had intended to seek him out.

"Why is that?"

Rafalo leaned back in his chair and regarded his claws thoughtfully.

"I have a cousin. A very sweet and very foolish cousin."

Arcosta stared at him, completely at a loss, and Rafalo sighed.

"With a young and very romantic daughter. The girl... involved herself with an unsuitable male. And my cousin, instead of asking me to deal with him, made the mistake of telling her daughter that she was not to see him again."

"What happened?"

"What one might expect. She ran off with him."

"Perhaps they are truly mated—"

Rafalo snorted. "So much so that he immediately turned around and sold her to a Vedeckian slave trader."

"What?!" How could any male have performed such a dishonorable act?

"Since her mother at least had the sense to notify me of her escapade, I was already making inquiries. I managed to locate the slaver and offered a very large sum for her."

"You are going to buy her?" he asked, outraged at the suggestion.

"Believe me, it would not be my first choice. But if I alert the Patrol and they go in after her..." Rafalo suddenly looked his age. "Those cursed Vedeckians have too many informants. Such an attempt has gone wrong in the past. I couldn't take the chance that they would simply decide to eliminate her if they suspected the Patrol was after them."

"I see. Did you want me to accompany you when you go to retrieve her?"

"Not exactly." Rafalo's tail swished back and forth. "They were too suspicious to accept a bid from another Kissat. They think the buyer is a Ruijin male, and they are expecting an emissary to retrieve her. I intend to send you. I'll pay you well, of course," he added, naming a sum that would not only cover the remaining price for the property but provide a cushion for the first few months.

It was a tempting offer, but... "Why me?"

"Partially because she is on Maniga, and you are familiar with the planet."

Unfortunately. That had been his first attempt to settle down on a planet. He'd realized after the first month that Maniga was not for him, but he had committed to a one-year contract. The rest of the year had been as unpleasant as he anticipated, and he had been relieved to leave once his contract was complete.

"And also because you're a Cire," Rafalo added. "You are an honorable warrior who will not harm Neera or attempt to keep her for yourself."

"I am not a warrior," he protested.

"You were trained as one."

That was true enough. All Cires were trained in the arts of war from a very young age, but...

"That was a long time ago."

Before he left his dying planet, before he found solace in the rigorous, logical precision of engines and machinery.

"Have you forgotten your skills?" Rafalo raised a sardonic eyebrow. "And before you say yes, you should know that I have already seen the recording of the little incident in the cargo bay last week."

Arcosta shifted his feet uncomfortably. "Hirih was out of line."

"Undoubtedly. But your actions convinced me that you are the right male for this job."

Fuck. He knew better than to get involved, but when he had seen the big male terrorizing the smaller one, he had been unable to prevent himself from stepping in.

"And besides," Rafalo continued, "there should be little

HONEY PHILLIPS & BEX MCLYNN

need for any display of force. You simply go in, make the purchase, and leave. Notify me as soon as you are both away from there, and I will call in the Patrol."

Somehow, Arcosta didn't think it would be as simple as Rafalo made it sound. But to be so close to finally achieving his dream... And could he really leave a young female in danger?

"Very well. I will do it."

CHAPTER THREE

Arcosta looked around curiously as he drove up the street to the address he had been given. This was an older part of town, built before the new balena refining process had brought galactic attention to the previously insignificant planet of Maniga. The houses were large, on decent-sized plots, but most of them showed signs of decay and delayed maintenance. The popular areas now were the port and the complex of retail and luxury high-rises that had grown up around it.

His destination was no better maintained than the surrounding houses—a cracked walkway led through an over-grown garden to a lopsided front porch. He eyed the rotting boards suspiciously as he crossed to the front door. The house didn't even have a video interface, so he knocked loudly.

Please let this go smoothly, he thought. Despite Rafalo's praise of his fighting skills, he found no enjoyment in combat. Yet another reason he had chosen to leave Ciresia at his first opportunity.

After what seemed like an interminable wait, he knocked again, more forcefully this time. Another wait, and he was just contemplating looking for another door when he heard footsteps coming towards him.

"What do you want?" the male who answered the door demanded.

A Manigan, no longer in his first or even second youth, peered at him from beneath bushy orange brows. His equally bushy hair stood out around his head, and he was wearing a white coat stained in several places. He looked much more like a scientist than the slaver Arcosta had expected to find.

"I am not sure this is the right address. I am here to pick up a... package from a Captain Kwan."

"Yes, yes. It's about time."

"Are you Kwan?"

The male snorted in disgust. "Do I look like a Vedeckian? I'm Dr. Pagalan. Let's get this over with. I told Kwan that I didn't want anyone disrupting me for long."

Leaving the door open behind him, the older male stalked off down the hall. Arcosta shrugged, and followed him inside. If anything, the inside was even worse than the outside. None of the large rooms on either side of the wide hallway looked lived in. The few pieces of furniture that occupied them were dusty and broken.

"This way, this way," Dr. Pagalan demanded impatiently. He was standing in an open doorway with a set of stairs leading down. Arcosta's tail twitched, but he followed. Another door at the bottom of the stairs opened into a completely different environment. Through the glass panels lining one side of a utilitarian corridor, he could see a cluttered but well-equipped lab. A couple of additional scientists were scurrying about amongst the instruments and didn't look up as they passed. On the other side of the corridor, smaller windows revealed a series of exam rooms with an oddly clinical air. The male ignored them, marching halfway down the corridor before unlocking a door and throwing it open.

"This male has come to take you to your new master, girl. Time to go."

Arcosta joined him in the doorway, expecting another exam room. Instead he saw something more similar to a living area. A young Kissat female had sprung up from her chair, her claws raised defensively. She bore a strong enough resemblance to Rafalo that he was sure she was his target, but his attention was immediately drawn to the female next to her. He had never seen a female like her before. She had smooth, defenseless skin in a pale shade of cream. Short brown hair framed a face with wide grey eyes, an odd little nose, and an unexpectedly full, sensuous mouth. As their eyes met, he felt an electric shock run through his system. His tail lashed behind him as all his senses went on alert. He needed to get closer to her, to see if she was the source of the tantalizing fragrance lingering in the air. He had taken two steps into the room before he was aware that he had moved.

"Hurry up, girl," Pagalan demanded, abruptly reminding Arcosta of his mission.

"I don't want to go with him." The young female cast a desperate look at the enchanting stranger. "I want to stay with you, Claire."

Claire. He liked the sound of it, even though she was currently glaring at him as she put a protective arm around the girl. As she did, he saw the two additional occupants of the room. Two young Ragi children had been hiding against her side. They appeared almost identical, but one of them was studying him intently while the other scowled belligerently.

"Out of the question," Pagalan snapped. "You are of no use to me, and I have no intention of paying for your care."

Arcosta frowned at the Manigan male, surprised that he

was so eager to get rid of the young female. Even though not all races had been hit as badly as the Cire by the Red Death, there were far fewer females these days, and most males were happy to have one, let alone two. But if Pagalan didn't want the young female, perhaps he didn't want the other one either.

He took another quick look around the small room, noting the absence of external windows and remembering the locked doors. This was no place for a female.

"I would be prepared to take both of them off your hands," he found himself saying.

Fully aware of how the words would sound, he expected outrage, but instead, Claire gave him a thoughtful look.

"No," Dr. Pagalan said immediately. "The older one is one of my subjects."

Subjects? Horror washed over him as the lab across the corridor and the individual exam rooms took on a new significance. This mad male was experimenting with his female?

Anger replaced his horror. His first impulse was to simply force the scientist to release the females and the children. But Pagalan would not comply willingly and while the other scientists working in the lab didn't appear to represent much of a threat, they were certainly capable of alerting the authorities if a fight ensued. The fact that they were harboring female slaves might deter them, but it might not. The authorities on Maniga were notoriously corrupt.

He forced himself to be calm and think logically. This was not the time for brute force—he needed more information, which meant he needed a reason to stay longer. He shrugged casually.

"What a shame. My employer has paid me well—very well —for this job, and I find the idea of a slave of my own rather appealing."

Claire's speculative look turned to one of disgust, and he

24

had to fight back the impulse to retract his words. Dr. Pagalan, on the other hand, looked intrigued.

"I see. You have some credits to burn."

Once again, he forced himself to nod, despite the avaricious gleam in the scientist's eyes.

"Did you have something specific in mind? The female child might be available. For the right price."

"You can't do that!" Claire cried, and Neera echoed her protest.

"No!" The young boy threw his arms around his sister.

Dr. Pagalan didn't react to the protests, his eyes on Arcosta. He forced his face to remain impassive, even though his tail was twitching angrily.

"She is very young," he said casually.

"But her value will only increase. The Ragi are an attractive race. When she reaches mating age, you will have interested purchasers lined up at your door. Or you may make use of her yourself. Or both."

"I wish to examine her."

The scientist shrugged. "Go ahead."

"No," Claire protested, pulling the child behind her.

Dr. Pagalan raised a device, and to Arcosta's horror, he recognized it as the control for a shock collar. He had to sink his nails into his palms to resist the impulse to strangle the male where he stood.

"You will not interfere," Pagalan said coldly.

Claire glared furiously but didn't move again as he approached. She was so close to him that her delicious fragrance filled his head, and it took all his training to concentrate on the two children instead. The boy had his arm tightly around his sister's shoulders, but the girl didn't flinch as he knelt in front of her. Big dark eyes studied him intently as his tail curved around and gently touched her cheek.

"Hello, little one. My name is Arcosta. What's your name?"

"Her name is Juni," Claire said quickly. "She doesn't speak."

"An advantage in a female," Dr. Pagalan muttered. "Are you satisfied?"

A smile flickered across Juni's face, and she patted his tail with a tiny hand before he rose to his feet. As he did, his tail escaped his control long enough to encircle Claire's wrist. He heard her breath catch, and he desperately wanted to pull her closer, to reassure her that he meant no harm. Instead, he forced himself to release her and rejoin the scientist.

"I am willing to discuss the matter," he said coolly.

"Excellent. Come with me."

Dr. Pagalan led him down the corridor and into what was clearly his office. The space was as cluttered and unkempt as everything else Arcosta had seen. More jovial now that he anticipated a profit, the scientist cleared a stack of books off a chair and gestured for Arcosta to take a seat.

"Tea? Or would you prefer something stronger?"

He didn't want anything from this male, but he had a part to play.

"Tea would be fine."

Dr. Pagalan nodded and rummaged around until he located two none-too-clean cups. Once the tea had been poured, he sat down behind his desk and stared at Arcosta thoughtfully. Something about the other male's gaze made his skin crawl, so he turned to practical matters.

"Do you speak for the other scientists?" he asked casually.

"Other scientists? Oh, you mean my assistants. Not a brain in the lot of them." Pagalan waved a dismissive hand.

Excellent. If the males he had seen in the lab were simply hired help, they would probably be leaving at the end of the day.

As much as he hated to do it, he forced himself to ask, "Then how much do you want for the child?"

The male assumed a pious air. "Perhaps I was too hasty. The child is like a daughter to me."

"If you're not interested..." He started to rise.

"No, no. In my line of work sacrifices must be made."

"What is your line of work?"

"The pursuit of knowledge. I intend to remedy some of the damage done by the Red Death." The scientist gave him another one of those discomforting looks. "You are from Ciresia, are you not?"

"Yes."

"And your race lost all its females?"

"Yes."

Pagalan hummed speculatively. "So many males desperate for a mate. I bet they would be willing to pay anything..."

His first reaction was outrage that anyone would attempt to purchase a female, but that was exactly what he had proposed. He forced his face to remain impassive and hoped the scientist wouldn't understand why his tail was lashing angrily.

"Not *any* price," he said coldly. "But a reasonable amount."

The negotiations began. He hadn't originally intended to go through with the purchase, but in the end he decided to proceed. It would allow him to get the girl away from this terrible place and make it easier for him to retrieve Claire and the boy.

Dr. Pagalan beamed with smug satisfaction once they finally agreed on a price and Arcosta transferred the credits. It had taken most of his savings—the shop was now completely out of reach—but he didn't regret it. As he passed the tablet back to Dr. Pagalan, he felt a sharp sting on his palm.

"I do apologize. This ring is a family heirloom, but the

prongs are damaged." The scientist showed him the sharp point on the elaborate ring he was wearing.

"No matter." For a moment, he had been concerned that the scientist was trying to drug him, but the sting was already fading and he felt no different than normal.

Dr. Pagalan rubbed his hands together, looking even more pleased with himself. "Now, if you'll just collect your purchases, I have work to be done."

CHAPTER FOUR

Claire stared at the door to their room as it closed behind Dr. Pagalan and the strange male. When it had opened and she had seen the big green alien standing next to the scientist, her first reaction had been curiosity rather than fear. He was huge, his tight black shirt, clinging to massive shoulders and a broad chest, tucked into equally tight pants that clung to thick thighs and... She hastily snatched her gaze away from the prominent bulge between his legs and focused on his face. His skin was patterned in soft shades of jade and emerald with a subtle raised texture. Rather than hair, thick ridges ran back over his head and down onto his shoulders. His eyes were a crystalline black without whites, but when their eyes met, she had felt the strangest shock of recognition, as if she knew him.

His words should have horrified her—first his offer to purchase her, and then, even more appallingly, the possibility that he was going to purchase Juni. But then he had stepped towards them and he had spoken to the little girl in that deep gentle voice. Her brain couldn't reconcile the difference between that voice and the callous offer. And when his tail curved around her wrist, warm and covered with intriguing little nubs, there had been a comfort to that touch she hadn't expected.

"He can't take Juni—he can't." Beni clutched her arm with desperate fingers, his small face panicked. "She needs me."

She put her arms around him, but as much as she wanted to reassure him and promise that the twins wouldn't be separated, she knew she would be helpless to prevent it. To her surprise, Juni took his hand. The girl looked nowhere near as worried as she would have expected. Despite Juni's silence, Claire was well aware of how much she noticed about her surroundings. The girl leaned her head against her brother's, and his anxiety gradually calmed, although he still scowled up at Claire.

"She says it's all right," he said begrudgingly. "But I don't like it."

"Juni thinks it's all right?" she asked, well aware that Beni and Juni communicated in some silent way she didn't understand.

The little girl looked up at her and nodded solemnly.

"It might be all right for her, but it's definitely not all right for me." Neera had been pacing back and forth, but she came and threw herself down next to them. "I don't want to be sold."

Despite Neera's petulant tone, Claire could see she was close to tears.

"You said your cousin would be looking for you, right? Maybe he's closer than you think." She did her best to sound reassuring, and Neera gave her a tremulous smile.

"I know he'll find me, eventually. But what if he's too late? I've never..." Sharp little teeth closed on her lower lip, and Claire remembered Kwan's comment about her virginity. Her own helplessness infuriated her.

"Just try and concentrate on the fact that he's coming for you. Hang onto that, no matter what."

The words sounded inadequate, even to herself, but Neera straightened her shoulders and nodded.

"Maybe it's a good sign that my new owner sent a Cire for me."

"A Cire?"

"The warrior with Dr. Pagalan. They have a reputation as an honorable race."

How honorable could they be if this one is involved with slavers? And yet there was something about him that made her want to trust him.

She didn't respond to Neera's statement, and the four of them sat huddled together until the door opened again. Dr. Pagalan looked triumphant, but Arcosta's face was inscrutable. He focused on her immediately, and remembering Juni's words, she thought—hoped—that he was trying to reassure her.

The little girl took Claire's arm and wrapped it around her brother before kissing them both and walking over to Arcosta. She looked up at him solemnly and he returned her gaze. Whatever she saw there must have reassured her because she raised her arms. Without hesitating, he reached down and lifted her up against his chest. She looked impossibly tiny, and Beni started to struggle in Claire's arms.

"Shh," she whispered softly. "Remember what she said."

He stopped struggling but she felt a hot tear drop onto her arm.

"You too, girl," Dr. Pagalan ordered.

Despair crossed Neera's face, but she looked at Juni, raised her chin, and crossed slowly to the waiting males.

"Well, go on. I have work to do." Dr. Pagalan started to give the Cire an impatient shove, but one look from the big male made him pull back. "I fulfilled my end of the bargain."

Arcosta looked as if he was about to speak, but after one final look at Claire, he took Neera's arm and left. At least it looked as if he took it gently, as if he were escorting her rather than taking her away. She suddenly wanted to call them back, to put her own hand on that big arm and let him take her out of here, but there was no hope for her.

Beni's bravery crumpled, and he started to sob. Taking care of him was more important than giving into her own desolation, and she started to rock him, murmuring meaningless reassurances.

"Tell him to be quiet," Dr. Pagalan snapped. "I should have thrown him in with his sister, the whiny little brat."

She glared at him. "Then go after him."

"I have work to do." He gave Beni a speculative look. "Although now that I know there's a market..."

He didn't complete his sentence before storming back out of the room and locking the door behind him, but the threat was clear. Her heart already ached at Juni's loss. What was she going to do if she lost Beni as well? The twins had been the only thing that kept her going over these last terrible months, and she loved them as if they were her own children. Fate seemed determined to make sure that she would never be a mother, but for Beni's sake she did her best to hide her sorrow. They went through their normal evening routine, and then she cuddled him until he fell into an uneasy sleep. He usually slept with his arms around his sister, and he clung to the meager pillow she had given him as a substitute with all his strength.

Sleep did not come as easily for her, and she was still awake when Dr. Pagalan returned, his eyes gleaming with that fanatical light she had come to dread. He had some new test in mind, but she was too despondent to protest as he took her to one of the exam rooms. A little to her surprise, he merely repeated his usual procedure—a scan and then an injection into her abdomen.

He actually rubbed his hands together gleefully as he finished.

"If this works, they'll have to award me the Ranut medal."

"If what works?"

"You couldn't possibly understand."

But despite his condescending tone, he immediately began rambling about zygotes and mating and chromosomal pairs as he took her back to the room. Unfortunately, he was right. She didn't understand what he was talking about, and his enthusiasm only made her more uneasy. The last time he thought he had a breakthrough and it had failed, he had subjected her to a long series of painful tests. He made it quite clear that he blamed her for the failure and had been unnecessarily sadistic.

This is going to be my life, she thought she lay on her bunk and stared up at the ceiling. Pain and tests, and even if by some chance Dr. Pagalan did succeed, it would only mean another loss. For the first time since those dreadful days after the accident when she woke up in the hospital alone, the thought of ending her life resurfaced.

And then all the lights went out.

CHAPTER FIVE

Arcosta escorted Neera out of the scientist's house, still holding Juni against his chest. The tiny girl felt right there, as if she belonged to him, but he knew it was only an illusion. She was, however, his responsibility, and he would make sure no harm came to her until he could find a suitable family to raise her and her brother.

Without glancing back at the house, he placed the females in the vehicle he had hired. At the time, he hadn't considered the cost, but now that his credit balance was close to zero, he regretted the expense. Even though he hadn't detected any signs of surveillance on the outside of the house, he drove away without a backwards glance. The labs did have extensive security monitoring, and he didn't want to make a foolish mistake. He would have to take care when he returned later that night.

"Where are you taking us?" Neera glared at him, trying to sound defiant, but he could hear her voice trembling. Juni was sitting quietly in the older girl's lap, and now she patted Neera's arm comfortingly. The child seemed completely unperturbed by the separation—the temporary separation, he reminded himself.

"I have a safe place to wait." As soon as he realized he would have to return, he had started considering the possibilities. He didn't want to risk more than one trip to ship. His lips curved as he shot a glance at her fancy clothes and unruffled fur. "Although I do not think you are going to like it."

She waved her hand impatiently. "Wait for what?"

His natural inclination was to keep his plans confidential, but he wanted her, wanted both of them, to know that he had no intention of abandoning their friends.

"Until dark. I'm going back to get Claire and Beni."

Juni nodded complacently, but Neera gaped at him.

"Why? Are you going to steal them as well? So you can make even more of a profit out of selling all of us?"

"No one is selling anyone," he growled. "Your cousin sent me after you."

Her mouth opened even further. "Rafalo? I don't understand. If that's true, why take Juni? And why go back for the others?"

"Do you really think I would leave any female, let alone children, in the hands of that madman?"

He suspected that if she had been capable of changing color the way human females did, she would have blushed. Instead, she shook her head rapidly.

"No, of course... I mean..." She pulled herself together and frowned at him. "Why wouldn't you? No one else seems to care."

"I am Cire," he said firmly, but he was aware that he wasn't being completely honest. He would have gone back, for the children and for any female, of course, but the urgency beating at him to rescue Claire was more than just the actions of an honorable male. He needed to protect her in a way he didn't quite understand. Leaving her in that house had taken all of the self-discipline he had learned over the years. Even now, he wanted to return.

Instead, he sighed and continued down the hill.

The old neighborhood led into a transitional retail area between the residential section and the new part of the city. Many of the houses remained, but they had been converted into small restaurants and quirky stores. He turned in next to the restaurant his friend had worked at when he had been living on Maniga. As he had noted on his way through, it was still operating. Lights were already on inside as the staff began to prepare for the evening rush, but that meant they would not be looking outside. He drove the small vehicle down the narrow lane next to the kitchen garden, and pulled in behind the storage building at the back of the lot. The day's deliveries would have been completed and any produce already gathered. No one would be coming back here until the following morning.

He urged the females out of the vehicle before pulling a tarp over it. It wouldn't disguise it from a serious search, but it wouldn't be immediately recognizable to a casual glance. Once it was covered, he urged the two of them into the small shed attached to the rear of the storage building. Neera recoiled in disgust.

"What is this place?" She looked at the rows of nesting boxes, and her eyes widened. "You want us to wait in a gosa pen?"

"You will be safe here. No one will be back here until the morning, and we will be long gone by then."

"Wouldn't a hotel be better?"

"No. Hotels ask questions. People notice who comes and goes. And their locks are easy to break."

She bit her lip again, then nodded. "I understand."

He turned to look at Juni and found her carefully lifting one of the gosas out of its nesting box. Why hadn't he been paying closer attention? The small animals were valued for their eggs and their fur, but they had sharp claws and even sharper teeth. The males were also extremely protective and had a reputation for aggression when disturbed.

"Juni, don't," he said softly, reaching for the gosa. "They don't like..."

He was too late. The gosa had already opened its eyes. Arcosta started to dive for it, but it turned its head and looked up at Juni, shook out its fur, then nestled back down in her arms. The little girl gave him a beaming smile.

He debated trying to take the gosa away from her, but the animal seemed content in her arms and he was reluctant to deny her that small comfort.

"Please watch out for her while I'm gone," he said quietly to Neera.

The girl gave a snort of what seemed like genuine amusement. "Why do I think it should be the other way around? But of course I will. Are you leaving us?"

"I have some preparations to make." Night was already closing in on them, but he saw her eyes gleam. "I'm not sure how long it will be, but I will be back."

He started to leave, then turned back.

"Wait for me until daybreak. If we have not returned, take the vehicle and go to the landing field. The ship is the *Dark Star*. The captain is one of your cousin's males. He will return you to your home." *I hope.* Captain Lokar had seemed pleasant enough, but he was a scavenger, and Arcosta didn't know him well enough to know if he would value honoring a promise over profit.

He also wondered if he had made a mistake in telling the girl. What if she decided to leave as soon as he was out of sight?

"I will wait as long as possible," she said, and he could hear the sincerity in her voice.

Juni stopped cooing over her new friend for a second and looked up at him. She nodded her head as well, and even in the dimness he saw the confidence on her face. He just hoped that it wasn't misplaced.

Four hours later, he carefully adjusted his cramped position. He was crouched in the line of overgrown bushes separating Pagalan's property from his neighbor. He had already seen two of the lab assistants leave, but that meant one remained—the large Sukonan. It was possible that he had left before Arcosta arrived, but it was also possible that he lived at the house.

Thoughts of what might be happening inside urged him to proceed with his plan, but he knew it had the best chance of succeeding if there was no one else present other than Dr. Pagalan. He checked his chronometer. Another hour until midnight. He would wait until then.

Only a few minutes later, the back door opened and the Sukonan sauntered out.

"Cheap ass bastard," the male was muttering to himself. "He expects me to take the night shift but doesn't want to pay for it. Well, what you don't know doesn't hurt me, Doctor."

Despite his belligerent demeanor, the male cast several cautious looks back over his shoulder as he made his way down the path and out through a rusty gate, only a few feet away from Arcosta's hiding place. Despite the gate's decrepit appearance, it opened and closed silently, and he suspected that it wasn't the first time it had been used.

Unless someone had arrived while he was gone, the house should now be empty except for the scientist. He crept across the back garden, keeping to the shadows even though his additional surveillance still hadn't revealed any exterior cameras. A large utility box was located next to the back door. It was locked, but he used a small tool from his belt to pick the lock. He wasn't surprised to find the inside as disheveled as the house. Nothing was labeled, and additional power sources had been connected to the main inputs with no regard to the capacity of the circuits.

Scorch marks indicated places where the system had overloaded previously, and a grim smile crossed his lips. Dr. Pagalan might even assume that the power going out was simply another failure of the overloaded system. He had originally planned to cut the wires, but rather than leave such an obvious trace, he wrapped a rubber guard around the end of his tool and touched the other end to one of the circuits. There was a satisfying spark, then the hum of power stopped and the few lights there were on in the house went out.

Perfect.

As he had hoped, the back door operated on an electronic lock just as the front door had done. With the power out, it opened at his touch. He moved silently along the corridor until he came to the door leading to the basement lab. It too opened easily, then he descended into the darkness below.

Upstairs, enough dim moonlight had penetrated that he was not entirely blind, but even his enhanced eyesight couldn't penetrate total blackness. He had a small light, but he would rather not use it unless absolutely necessary. Fortunately, he had memorized which door led to Claire's room so he would be able to find his way.

As he opened the second door, the darkness was replaced by a dim red glow that illuminated the lab area. *Fuck.* Dr. Pagalan must have a backup generator for this area. He paused for a second, but he couldn't hear anyone moving around so he began edging silently down the corridor.

The emergency lighting gave everything an eerie glow,

enhanced by the murmur of equipment in the lab itself. It reminded him of the horror stories his older brother tried to frighten him with long ago, before the Red Death became the ultimate horror and took his brother, along with the rest of his family.

When he put his hand on the door to Claire's room, it didn't open. As he tried it a second time, he remembered Dr. Pagalan pressing his thumb against the lock. *Damn.* He had hoped that the thumbprint recognition would also have failed, but it was either on a separate system or powered by the emergency generator. He would have to break down the door, and that would not be a silent process.

He also didn't want to take a chance on hurting Claire or the boy, so he moved over to the observation panel and looked inside. They were both sitting on the bed, their eyes wide and Claire's arms tight around the boy. Even in the eerie red light, she looked beautiful, but she also looked scared and his tail twitched with the urge to reassure her. He gave her what he hoped was a comforting smile, then pointed to himself and then to the door. She gave a shaky nod.

"What are you doing back here?" a voice demanded impatiently, and he turned to find the scientist marching towards him.

Fuck. He had been so distracted that he hadn't heard Dr. Pagalan emerge from his office.

"I am coming to take what is mine," he said calmly.

To his surprise, the scientist gave him a triumphant smile before frowning again. "That's quite out of the question. Even if you had returned with a million credits, my work is far more important than your lust."

Lust? He wasn't quite sure what he felt, but he knew it went far beyond mere physical attraction.

"Now leave here at once, before I call the authorities."

Arcosta's heart sank as the scientist pulled out a portable communication device. The house lines would have been disconnected when the power failed, but it would have no effect on the device. The foolish male was still coming towards him as if his threats would be enough to deter Arcosta. He closed the remaining gap in two quick steps, his tail whipping out to dislodge the communication device and send it smashing into the wall with a satisfying crash.

He grabbed the front of Dr. Pagalan's disreputable lab coat and lifted him off the ground.

"I said I have come for what is mine."

"But you—"

The words cut off abruptly as Arcosta's fist connected with the male's chin, and he collapsed. *Pitiful.* He started to drop the scientist, then remembered the lock. He dragged him back down the hallway and pressed his thumb against the lock. The door opened with a satisfying click, and he dropped the other male. Claire came hurrying out, Beni in her arms, and his tail immediately wrapped around her waist. To his relief, she didn't protest. She even seemed to lean into him.

"Is he dead?" she whispered, looking down at Dr. Pagalan's body.

"No. Would you like him to be?"

"I..." She hesitated, looking at Beni, then shook her head. "Killing him would make us no better than him."

"I assure you, there is no comparison between you," he said dryly. "But it might be better to let the Patrol handle him, once we are safely away from here."

While he would suffer no guilt from ending the scientist's life, he didn't like the idea of killing a defenseless male. He shoved the unconscious male into Claire's room and locked the door. The Patrol could determine how to get him out. Right now, Arcosta was more concerned with getting Claire and Beni safely away from the lab.

"We should go. If there is an automated system monitoring the power, they may send someone to check on the outage."

"What about Neera and Juni?"

"They are safe, but we should get back to them as quickly as possible."

Her step slowed. "And then what?"

"We get the hell off this planet," he said, urging her to speed up. Instead, she came to a complete halt.

"Who are you? Why are you doing this?"

"Neera's cousin Rafalo sent me."

"The one she was talking about?" Some of the tension left her slender body. "Oh, thank goodness. I told her that he would send someone. But why me? Why the children?"

Several answers rose to his lips, but this was neither the time nor the place.

"An honorable male would not leave you—any of you—here," he said truthfully.

She gave him an uncertain look, but to his relief she started walking again.

"Neera said that the Cire have a reputation for behaving honorably."

"I am glad to hear that."

He meant what he said, but as he urged them up the stairs and out through the rear door, he also felt an increasing sense of dismay. As much as he was drawn to her, would an honorable male pursue her under such conditions? He didn't know what had occurred in the lab, but she was no doubt traumatized. She had put her trust in him, and he could not betray that trust, he decided ruefully. He would have to wait until she was confident in her safety.

Despite his resolutions, it took three tries before he could force his tail to release her. An effort that wasn't helped by the fact that she immediately turned to look up at him. For a moment, he thought she would say something, but then Beni finally spoke. He had been clinging silently to Claire the entire time, but now he looked up at Arcosta, his lips trembling.

"I want Juni."

"You will be with her soon," he promised. "Will you let me carry you? It will be faster."

The small brows drew together, but then the boy nodded. "You carried Juni."

"I did. She came to no harm with me, and neither will you."

The boy nodded again and held out his arms. Claire reluctantly passed him over, then gave him a rueful smile.

"I hate to admit it, but he does get heavy."

His unruly tail was back around her waist, and he gave her a quick squeeze before pulling it away again. Then he took her hand, and set off at the fastest pace he thought she could manage.

CHAPTER SIX

Claire did her best to keep up as Arcosta led them rapidly along the narrow street. It ran behind the largest estates she had glimpsed so briefly when Kwan had brought her to Dr. Pagalan. They still reminded her of Victorian-style mansions with their ornate moldings and odd little turrets emerging from unexpected places. The moon—no, two moons—were only faintly visible through the heavy cloud cover, but they cast enough light for her to make out the cobblestones beneath her feet. A cool breeze brushed across her cheek, carrying an oddly metallic scent as well as a delicious spicy fragrance that seemed to come from Arcosta. She didn't even realize she was crying until he turned around to look at her.

"What is it, Claire? What's wrong?"

"It's just... I was beginning to think I would never get out of there. That I would spend my whole life in the lab. Never get to see the sky or feel fresh air again."

His tail circled her waist as it had done earlier, and he pulled her gently against his chest. She didn't resist. His big warm body and that oddly comforting scent surrounded her as she cried. Beni leaned over and put his small arms around her neck.

"Don't cry, Claire," the little boy whispered.

She scrubbed her hands across her cheeks, wiping away the tears, and took a step back. Arcosta's tail lingered for a moment longer before dropping away.

"You are free now, kimati," he said solemnly. "I will do everything in my power to ensure that you stay free."

Other than his assurance that Rafalo had sent him, she had no real reason to trust him. He could be planning to sell all of them, just like the male Neera had so blindly trusted. But even though her rational side argued caution, looking up at those dark eyes, even more mysterious in the dim moonlight, she believed him.

"Thank you. Thank you for getting us out of there."

He simply nodded, then took her hand and started walking again. *Thank God it was downhill*, she thought as she struggled to keep up with him once more. She had abandoned her exercise routine after she left the hospital, and the time spent underground in the lab had done nothing to improve her stamina. Pride, as much as anything, kept her moving, even as her legs started to ache and the strap on her flip-flops rubbed painfully between her toes. Beni kept looking back at her over Arcosta's shoulder, making sure that she was still there, and she found herself envying him. What would it be like to be carried in those massive arms?

Don't be ridiculous, she scolded herself. She might have decided to trust him, but it would be foolish to think this was anything more than a temporary acquaintance.

The alley emptied into a maze of small back streets, but Arcosta never hesitated, winding his way with complete confidence although he kept a watchful eye on their surroundings.

"Do you know this area?" The question came out in a breathless rush, and he slowed his pace as he nodded.

"I had a friend who worked in one of the restaurants down here."

A friend? She had a sudden vision of a tall, athletic female and felt a completely inappropriate flash of jealousy.

"I used to visit him when I was off shift. It hasn't changed much."

Oh. He meant a male friend. Hoping that her burning cheeks weren't visible in the moonlight, she managed another question.

"Off shift?"

"I had a work contract here on Maniga several years ago." He didn't supply any additional details, but returned to scanning their surroundings.

They turned down one street, then another, before finally pausing in front of a narrow wooden door set in a brick wall. She watched in dismay as he tried the handle and found the door locked, but he didn't seem bothered. He passed Beni over to her, then pulled a small metal wire from his belt. A few quick movements, and then the door opened with a quiet click.

As she followed him through the doorway, some of her initial doubts started to return. What kind of male knew how to pick a lock so easily? And for that matter, how had he known how to cut the power and break into the lab? Then again, Neera had indicated that her cousin wasn't exactly a law-abiding citizen. Did it really matter as long as he was helping them?

"Juni is waiting," Beni said, interrupting her thoughts as he started squirming in her arms, trying to get down.

Arcosta nodded, pointing to what looked like some type of animal pen. "In there."

He'd put Neera and Juni in a cage? She gave him an

outraged look, even as she lowered Beni to the ground and he took off. The door to the pen opened before he reached it, Juni beaming at him as Neera appeared behind her and grabbed for the door. The girl relaxed as she saw them coming towards her.

"Thank Hebra it's you. She had the door open before I realized she was moving."

Claire smiled at her as she kneeled down to put her arms around both twins. Beni had his own arms protectively around Juni, who was holding a...

"What is that?"

The small animal had long ears like a rabbit, but it had a sharp, pointed face and a long, slender body. Pink fur covered most of its body, but two long white stripes ran down its back to a short, stubby little tail.

"His name is Lukat. He's Juni's friend," Beni said happily.

"I'm glad it—he—could keep her company," she said gently. "But you need to put him back now, Juni."

Two pairs of identical dark eyes fastened on her face, and then Juni shook her head.

"Juni thinks he should come with us," Beni translated unnecessarily.

She looked up at Arcosta, seeking his support, but he was smiling down at Juni.

"Now that he's out of the cage, he may run away," he warned the child.

"Juni says he won't." Beni seemed to think that was the end of the matter.

She frowned at Arcosta as she rose to her feet. "Are you sure about this?"

"No," he said with an unexpectedly charming smile. "But neither do I think this is the time or place for an argument. We need to get going."

He hesitated, looking first at her, then Neera. It was his turn to frown.

"What's wrong?"

"I will do my best to keep us away from others, but I suspect it will be impossible to get to the landing field without being seen at all. The two of you are too conspicuous. Attractive females always draw attention."

Attractive females? She felt her cheeks heating as she looked down at her shapeless gown and bare legs. The last thing she felt was attractive, but she decided he was probably just being kind. On the other hand, Neera was young and beautiful and would undoubtedly arouse that kind of attention.

Unfortunately, she couldn't see any way to disguise the girl, but before she could say as much, Arcosta strode over to a shapeless heap against the wall. He pulled off the covering to reveal an odd-looking car, but instead of urging them into the vehicle, he bent over the tarp with a knife he pulled out of his belt. In just a few minutes, he managed to create two rough but serviceable cloaks and handed one to each of them.

"These will help. Keep the hood pulled up over your head as much as possible."

As she started to obey, her fingers brushed against the hated shock collar. If Pagalan caught up with them, she would be helpless against it.

"Is there something you can do about this?"

"Forgive me. I should have removed it immediately."

He went to work with his lockpick, and a few seconds later, the collar fell away. Her neck felt strangely bare and vulnerable, and she wanted to cry again. Instead, she gave him a shaky smile as she murmured her thanks, and picked up the cloak again. The heavy material felt rough against her skin as she pulled it around her, but there was something reassuring about being concealed.

"What about the children? Do they need to be covered?"

"Cloaks won't disguise their size. Just keep them close to you. Although..."

He looked at Juni, still holding Lukat, and sighed before turning back to the tarp. This time, he rigged up something that looked rather like a small tote bag. It wasn't until he handed it to Juni and helped her place Lukat inside that Claire realized it was intended as a carrier.

Then he opened the door to the vehicle, rubbing his chin thoughtfully.

"This is going to be a tight fit for all of us, but the closer we can drive to the landing field, the less chance we have of encountering others."

"Then we'll just have to squeeze in," she agreed.

A few minutes later, she was regretting her blithe agreement. The vehicle was only designed for two people—two small people. Arcosta's big body more than filled the driver seat, and she was pressed tightly against his side with Beni on her hip. Neera was wedged against the other door, holding Juni and Lukat.

The position was far from comfortable, but despite that she was achingly conscious of even the smallest movement of his body as he drove the vehicle silently out into the street. She had never been this close to someone with such impressive muscles. Her husband Evan had never been particularly athletic, and his long hours at the office hadn't helped.

Arcosta's spicy scent filled her head, and to her shock, she felt her body starting to respond to his closeness. After all this time, this big alien male was the one to reawaken her long dormant body?

The vehicle jolted as they passed over a roughly paved section of road, and her breasts pressed against his side. Her nipples hardened into aching little points. She did her best to think of something—*anything*—else, but by the time he finally brought the vehicle to a halt, her whole body was on fire. As soon as he parked in a half-concealed alley, he threw open his door and jumped out. Why had he left so quickly? Had he realized she was aroused and was trying to get away from her?

But then he reached back in to assist her by taking Beni, and she caught a glimpse of the massive bulge between his thighs. He was undisputedly erect. *Oh.* Apparently, he had been just as affected by their closeness. In spite of their precarious situation, an unexpected and purely feminine feeling of satisfaction washed over her. She liked the fact that he found her desirable.

"This way," he said, his voice hoarse, as she and Neera climbed out of the vehicle.

She started to pick up Juni, but Arcosta intercepted her. He lifted both children into his arms, their small bodies tucked against his massive chest. They looked at home there, and her heart did an odd little flip before she forced herself to look away and turned to Neera.

"Come on. Let's get you home."

CHAPTER SEVEN

As Arcosta led the way through the thankfully deserted streets, he did his best to get his rebellious body under control. In spite of his unruly tail, he had managed to keep himself under control until their journey in the vehicle. But to have Claire's soft body pressed so closely against his. To hear the soft catch of her breath and feel the pebbled tips of her breasts against his side. To scent her arousal...

He was never going to regain control if he didn't stop remembering. He forced himself to concentrate on their surroundings instead. He had chosen this area deliberately. It was a little further from the landing field, but the businesses here closed earlier. The areas closer to the port tended to remain open around the clock, ready to supply the needs of the crews and passengers from the ships that arrived at all hours. He hadn't considered the fact that the additional distance would be hard on the females.

Once they reached the edge of the landing field, he asked them to wait in the shadows while he checked on the ship. It was just as well that he did. There was a Patrol ship parked next to the cruiser, and even as he watched, a uniformed officer marched Captain Lokar down the ramp. Under other circumstances, he would have been happy to see the law officers, but not now.

He faded back into the shadows between the buildings, returning to the females and children.

"What's wrong?" Claire asked immediately.

His tail automatically started to encircle her waist in a reassuring gesture, but he yanked it back.

"What makes you think something is wrong?"

"I can see it on your face."

Obviously, his efforts to remain impassive needed work.

"There is a Patrol ship parked next to our transport, and it looks as if they are arresting the captain. It is possible they are just taking him in for questioning, but either way, it means we have no immediate transportation off the planet."

Claire frowned at him. "You said the Patrol would take care of Dr. Pagalan. If they are some kind of law enforcement, doesn't that mean they would help us?"

"It is not quite that simple. I believe they would assist Neera to return home."

"But not us?"

"They might agree to return you to Earth, after they have erased this experience from your memory." This time, he couldn't restrain his tail. "But the children could not go with you."

He saw her swallow, but she lifted her chin defiantly. "I guess I had already accepted that. Especially if..."

"If what?"

She shook her head. "It's not important. But couldn't they help us find someplace safe?"

He hesitated, looking at the children, and saw the realization cross Neera's face.

"It is the children," he said gently. "If Pagalan is registered as their legal guardian, we have stolen them from him. And they would be returned to him."

Her arms closed defensively around the twins. "You have to be kidding. They're just lab experiments to him."

"I know. And I believe we could get them to investigate. But they would put the children in protective custody while they did so."

The dawning realization made her lips tremble. "Which would not be with me."

Both children huddled closer as he shook his head.

"I am afraid not. They would look for a more... stable environment."

Despite her obvious unhappiness, she looked down at the children. "Maybe that would be for the best. You could have a real home."

"No," Beni said emphatically, as his sister nodded. "We want to stay with you."

Her lips trembled again, but she smiled at them both. "I want to be with you too, but you deserve a home." She looked up at him, her eyes pleading. "Is there anywhere we could go that would be safe? Where I could make a living for us?"

He had to fight back the impulse to assure her that he would take care of all three of them. He had just spent all of his savings, and his tiny living space on the station had no room for family. But perhaps Rafalo would be willing to help, even if it meant that he would be working for the other male for the rest of his life. However, that didn't solve the immediate problem—how were the five of them going to return to the space station?

Or perhaps only four. He turned to Neera.

"I meant what I said, Neera. I believe the Patrol would return you to your mother."

"Would they?" The unexpected streak of cynicism sat

strangely on that young face. "Or would they assume that because I live on Rafalo's station, that I'm not worthy of their assistance?"

"I think your cousin may have prejudiced you too much against the Patrol. They can be a little officious, but in my encounters with them I have always found them to be fair."

"All it takes is one bad male. I know that now," the girl said defiantly, but he could see the hurt on her face. "I would rather stay with Claire and the twins."

He looked at Claire, and she nodded. Very well. That meant he needed to make plans for the five of them. He ran through the options. The best case scenario was that the Patrol would release the ship, but even then, it was quite possible that they would continue watching it. And if they couldn't use the ship, they would have to find another method of transport—which meant that he would need to barter his skills in order to provide passage. Unfortunately, that might not be a rapid process, and if Pagalan alerted the Vedeckians about what had happened once he regained consciousness, there was a good chance that they would be searching for them as well.

"Is this the only spaceport?" Claire asked softly.

"No, there is a smaller port down near the balena mines." His automatic response triggered a memory. Hadn't Tangari said that he was transporting balena oil? He hadn't specifically mentioned Maniga, but it was certainly one of the major export centers in this system. If he could locate Tangari, he was sure the other male would take them on board. And even if he couldn't, there was likely to be better-paying work for him at the mines than there would be in the city. The only problem was how to get there.

Due to the atmospheric conditions on Maniga, air travel was rare and expensive—far too expensive for his diminished savings. The most common means of transport between the mines and the city were the vehicle convoys that made the multi-day trip on a recurring schedule. The huge transports were primarily designed to transport the bulky, and less valuable, ore from the mines to the city, but many of the mine workers used them for the trip after their month-long shifts.

If he could find the right driver—one who wouldn't charge an outrageous amount and one who would keep his mouth shut about the presence of the females—it would be their best option. The vehicles departed from a huge facility at the far side of the landing field.

"I am afraid we have further to walk tonight. I will try and arrange transport to the other spaceport, but we will need to circle the landing field to get there."

Claire sighed but didn't protest, and Neera only nodded as he bent to pick up the twins. He did his best to keep his pace slow enough for them, but the transports departed at dawn and he didn't want to have to wait another day and risk further chance of discovery. By the time they reached the other side of the field, they were all clearly exhausted. He urged them into a half-empty storage facility next to the transport center to wait for him, then went to see if could find the right driver.

He had rejected most of them before he saw a grizzled male overseeing the fueling process. Udasi had been running this route back when Arcosta had been working on Maniga, and he had often traveled with him. The old male didn't take kindly to fools, but his acerbic barbs disguised a kind heart, and Arcosta trusted him completely.

"I am looking for a ride," he said briskly as he approached.

"Not interested. Try Blundar." Udasi jerked his head at the next transport without even looking around.

"I prefer experience."

The old male snorted, but he turned to look at him. His eyes widened.

"Arcosta? Is that you, boy? Never thought to see you on Maniga again."

"I never expected to be here. I can tell you all about it later, but I really do need a ride."

"Make an exception for you."

"It is not just for me." He checked to make sure that no one was in hearing distance. "I have two females and two children with me."

"Didn't think Cires went in for that sort of thing."

"It is not like that," he started to protest before he saw the twinkle in Udasi's eyes. "They need help."

"Yeah. All right."

He hesitated. "And I am low on funds."

Udasi peered at him from under his brows, then snorted. "Only got two cabins anyway."

"What?" When he'd traveled with him before, there had been at least ten.

The old male shrugged. "Tired of passengers. On the way into the city, they're already rowdy and looking for trouble. On the way back, they're hungover and they bitch and moan the whole way. Not worth it. I converted most of the cabins into cooling rooms to carry fresh produce back to the mines. More profit, less trouble."

Two cabins. From what he remembered, they were small at best, each one equipped with two narrow bunks. They had been designed for Manigans rather than someone his size. It still seemed like a better alternative than trying to hide in the city or find another driver as trustworthy as Udasi.

"We will take them."

CHAPTER EIGHT

Claire did her best not to protest as Arcosta left them in the hangar. Even though she had no doubt he would return, a pang of trepidation hit her as his tall figure disappeared through the open door. Their escape was clearly not working out as he had planned. But then again, he didn't seem dismayed. He had quickly discarded his original scheme and started to look for alternatives. She couldn't help thinking that her husband would have had a much harder time adapting.

Once Evan made a plan, he never wanted to change it. Even their attempt to expand their family had been one of his plans. When they first got married, they had agreed that they would have a child once he became a partner in his law firm. They hadn't discussed it after that, and soon she was as busy with her career as he was with his. Except for an occasional wistful pang on the rare occasions when she was around children, she hadn't given it much thought. But he had not forgotten. They had been driving home from the dinner celebrating the announcement of his partnership when he reminded her of their plan. Even though they were both approaching forty, he was determined to proceed. She hadn't been quite as sure at first, but once she considered it, she realized just how much she wanted a child.

But I lost my chance, she thought, her eyes stinging. Now she had Beni and Juni, and she was determined not to let anything happen to them. They were snuggled against her side, and she tightened her arms protectively around their small bodies as they waited.

By the time Arcosta returned, she was having trouble staying awake despite the danger. Only the pain in her feet and the ache in her legs was keeping her eyes open. The twins had already fallen asleep, one on either side of her with their heads on her legs and their hands joined. Neera also looked to be asleep, but her eyes opened when Arcosta walked in.

"I have arranged for transport." He actually looked somewhat hesitant. "It is somewhat... primitive, and I am afraid there are only two cabins."

Her pulse gave an unexpected flutter when he looked at her. Did that mean they would have to share?

"I will, of course, leave those for you and the children."

Wasn't that a noble—and slightly disappointing—answer?

"As long as I can lie down, I don't care," Neera said as she stood and stretched gracefully.

Despite her exhaustion, she looked as beautiful as ever. *Youth is definitely wasted on the young*, Claire thought wryly. She urged the twins to wake up, then stood, wincing when her feet touched the ground.

"What is wrong?"

Arcosta was at her side immediately.

"Flip-flops aren't exactly meant for long distances."

When he looked confused, she pointed to her feet. Even in the dim light, they looked swollen, and she could see the blisters around the toe straps. He hissed in dismay, and she expected that comforting tail to wrap around her waist. Instead, he lifted her into his arms. *Oh my.* When she had wondered how it would feel earlier, she hadn't even come close to imagining what being tucked against that broad chest with his spicy scent surrounding her would actually be like. He carried her as easily as he had carried the twins.

"But what about the twins?"

They were still on the crate, leaning against each other, eyes heavy and clearly exhausted.

"I can carry all of you," he said confidently. "Neera, will you hand them to me?"

The girl rolled her eyes in exactly the same way as every young girl Claire had ever known.

"Why do males always have to act so tough? I can carry the squirt if you take Juni."

Before he could object, she picked up Juni and dropped her into Claire's arms. Juni and her animal companion, who was poking his head out of his carrier and sniffing the air.

Claire sighed. "I hate to mention it, but I suspect Lukat needs a litterbox."

She half-expected Arcosta to huff, the way Evan would have if his plans weren't working out. Instead, he gave her his disarming grin.

"I will take care of it. After all of you are in the vehicle," he added firmly.

She didn't attempt to argue as he strode towards the open door of the hangar. Outside, huge flood lights illuminated a row of enormous vehicles. Each one had to be three stories high, their sides covered with thick sheets of riveted metal. Small porthole-like windows ran in a line close to the top. Instead of wheels, each vehicle had a series of tracks. Despite their tank-like appearance, she didn't see any signs of weaponry.

Although she wanted to ask him about them, he was

focused on their surroundings. She could hear the sound of voices and equipment, but they were coming from the other side of the vehicles. He waited a moment longer, then strode rapidly across the open concrete. From the easy way he moved, her weight didn't bother him at all.

She couldn't hear Neera, but when they reached a small ramp that led up over the tires to a doorway in the side of the vehicle, the girl was right behind them. She was breathing heavily, but she gave Claire a triumphant grin.

Arcosta didn't pause at the base of the ramp, striding up it and through the open doorway as quickly as if he had been on flat land. As soon as Neera and Beni followed, he pulled the door closed and she felt rather than heard him give a sigh of relief.

They were on a small catwalk overlooking a huge empty space. A few crates were tied in place along one wall, but otherwise the space was empty. All this room and that was the only cargo?

"The transports are primarily designed to bring ore to the city," Arcosta said softly. "The supplies they carry back don't take up much room."

She nodded, but he was already heading for another door at the end of the catwalk. Once inside, a narrow winding stair let up. And up. She heard Neera sigh.

"Wait here," Arcosta told the girl. "I will take Claire to her cabin and return for you and Juni."

Did that mean he was intending to carry Neera as well? She bit back an instinctive protest, knowing she was being self-ish. It helped that neither he nor Neera looked thrilled at the prospect. The girl shook her head.

"I can make it."

He looked at her, then nodded. "You go first, in case you need assistance."

It seems ridiculous that he would be able to prevent Neera from falling without dropping Claire and Juni in the process, but somehow she believed that he would manage.

The trip up the narrow stairs was painfully slow, but once again, he gave no sign of impatience and made no attempt to hurry Neera. By the time they reached the top, Claire could see the girl's legs shaking but she kept her head up. Arcosta led them down a corridor, then opened the door to a small, empty room. Claire looked around her in consternation. This was worse than their room in the lab.

Arcosta lowered her carefully to her feet, then pressed a hidden catch that made two narrow bunks unfold from the wall. Neera gave a grateful sigh as she put a sleepy Beni on the lower bunk before climbing gracefully into the upper. Juni wiggled out of Claire's arms and went to join her brother, still carrying the gosa.

"Let me take Lukat," Arcosta said quickly, then waited while Juni studied his face.

She gave him a tiny nod and handed over the carrier, climbed up on the lower bunk, wrapped her arms around her brother, and was immediately asleep.

"Come," Arcosta said, picking her up again. "We must tend to your wounds before they become infected."

She was about to argue with him, but he was right. The last thing she needed was to develop an infection. She looked over her shoulder at the twins, so small, even in the narrow bunk, and Neera gave her a sleepy smile.

"I'll watch over them. You two go have fun."

Neera's giggle followed her as Arcosta swept her out of the room.

"She has a strange idea of fun," she muttered, hoping she wasn't blushing again.

He looked down at her and smiled, but didn't comment as

he carried her through the door to the next cabin. The room was identical to the first, and Arcosta lowered the bottom bunk. He gently placed her on it, with Lukat in his carrier next to her. Fortunately, the gosa seemed to have gone back to sleep.

She expected he would need to leave to get water, but he opened another hidden panel to reveal a tiny bathroom. His shoulders actually touched both walls when he entered. *An educated woman shouldn't be so easily impressed by sheer size and strength*, she thought, but that didn't prevent the little flicker of arousal she felt as she watched his muscles flex beneath the tight shirt. She was still staring at him when he turned and caught her watching.

Their eyes met and another, much stronger wave of attraction washed over her. The air seemed to hum between them, but then his gaze dropped to her feet and the tension dissipated. She wasn't the least bit disappointed, she told herself.

But then he kneeled at her feet and a big warm hand closed over her bare calf as he raised her foot. She barely kept herself from moaning when he gently kneaded the aching muscles.

"That feels good," she whispered.

"Yes," he agreed, his eyes focused on where his hand was wrapped around her leg. Then the skin across his cheekbones seemed to darken, and he focused on her feet, carefully removing the flip-flops. Using a wet cloth he'd retrieved from the bathroom, he carefully cleaned her injuries. Despite the exquisite gentleness, she had to clench her fists in the thin blanket to prevent herself from flinching. His tail came up to circle her wrist comfortingly as he applied an herbal-smelling ointment. When he was finally finished, they both breathed a sigh of relief.

"It would be better if you could soak them," he said, studying the swollen flesh. "I wish there was a bathing pool on board."

"Me too," she agreed, thinking wistfully of the big cast iron tub in her Colorado cottage.

"I will see what I can find." He stood, looming impossibly tall in the small cabin. "As well as a litterbox for Lukat. I will return as quickly as possible."

Despite his words, he looked down at her for a long second before he finally turned towards the door. She had a sudden foolish urge to ask him not to leave, but she kept silent.

The cabin door closed behind him, and the small space instantly seemed cold and empty. *I'm an independent woman*, she reminded herself. Instead of lusting after Arcosta, she would be better off trying to think of a way to support herself and the twins. She leaned back against the mattress, surprisingly comfortable despite its thinness, and closed her eyes as she tried to come up with a plan. Exhaustion swept over her in long, drugging waves. She was asleep before he returned.

CHAPTER NINE

Arcosta found Udasi at the controls, doing a last-minute check. The convoy would set out at dawn, and the sky was already beginning to lighten beneath the heavy clouds that always covered the sky. He cackled madly when Arcosta asked him about a bathtub.

"Got some fancy ideas since you left."

"It is for my female—*the* female," he said stiffly.

Udasi eyed him with a gaze that was as sharp as ever despite his age, but to Arcosta's surprise, he didn't comment on his slip.

"Got a storage bin next to my workshop. Can't promise you'll find anything suitable, but you were always good at making do."

"Thank you."

He turned to go, then hesitated. Udasi seemed unusually alert, his eyes scanning the landing field continuously.

"Is something wrong?"

"Nah. Lot of newcomers on this trip. Just making sure they aren't going to fuck everything up."

"Compared to you, everyone is a newcomer."

Udasi cackled again. "You got that right. Go on now. Make your lady her bathtub."

Well aware that his cheeks were darkening, he did his best to ignore the comment and left without arguing. The storage room had a wealth of parts, but nothing of an adequate size for bathing. The best he could find was a circular drum that would be large enough for her to put her feet in. He cut off the top third to use as a litterbox, found some old packing material to use as litter, and carried everything back to the cabin. He stopped on the way to check on Neera and the twins and found them all sound asleep.

Claire was also asleep, her delicate body curled on the open bunk. He considered waking her, but even in the short time he had been gone, the antibiotic had started to work. Her wounds no longer looked quite as inflamed, and he decided to let her sleep.

Lukat poked his head up from the carrier and chittered softly. Arcosta poured the packing material into the makeshift litterbox and breathed a sigh of relief when the gosa promptly made use of it. At least he wouldn't be constantly cleaning up after it. Lukat hopped back up on the bunk and curled up next to Claire. He wished he could do the same. Despite the thrum of arousal running through his veins, he would be content just to hold her.

I should leave, he thought, but he couldn't make himself go. Instead, he settled down on the floor, his back against the door. He would keep watch, he decided, so if her feet troubled her and she woke, he would be close at hand.

A short time later, he heard the engines turn over and felt the vibration as the vehicle began moving. Even after all this time, it was a familiar sensation and he smiled, unexpectedly at peace. They were on their way out of the city, and Claire and the children were safe.

He didn't realize he had fallen asleep until a soft noise made him look up. Claire was peeping at him from the bunk, her eyes smiling. Her face was flushed from sleep and her hair disheveled, but she looked beautiful. More than that, she looked... happy, he realized. More relaxed than she had been since they met.

"That doesn't look very comfortable," she said, then yawned. "Is it time to get up?"

He automatically glanced at the dim greyish light coming in through the porthole, then shook his head.

"It is not necessary. The vehicle will travel throughout the day and make camp late in the afternoon. You may as well sleep while you have the opportunity."

"I should check on the children."

"I did when I returned. They are sleeping soundly."

She yawned again. "I suppose you're right." She regarded him thoughtfully for a moment, then gave a decisive nod.

"I have an idea. Why don't we fold up the bunks and put both mattresses on the floor? At least it would give you more room to spread out."

"What about you?" he protested, even as his unruly cock jerked at the idea of being so close to her.

She peeped at him from under her lashes, grey eyes sparkling with mischief.

"I think I can control myself."

She wasn't the one he was concerned about. *I am an honorable Cire*, he reminded himself. *I will remain in control.*

When she tried to stand up so he could retrieve the mattress, she hissed when her feet hit the ground. He immediately snatched her up in his arms.

"Do not try to stand."

In his haste, he had lifted her against the front of his body. Her soft flesh pressed against him, and he could feel the heated points of her nipples branding his chest. Their faces were level, and he watched in fascination as a tiny pink tongue swept across that sensual mouth.

"I haven't said thank you," she whispered, then leaned forward and pressed her incredibly soft lips against his.

Astonishment held him motionless, too shocked to respond, and he felt her stiffen and pull back. Blunt little teeth closed on her plump lower lip as pink washed over her face.

"I'm sorry. I—"

He didn't give her a chance to continue. He pressed his lips against hers, hard enough that she gave a little squeak, and he gentled his touch. Her body relaxed, and then that delicate little tongue shyly slipped into his mouth.

Her taste flooded his senses, and he forgot that he was a Cire, forgot that he was an honorable warrior. He wanted —*needed*—more. His hand cupped her head, fingers buried in the soft silky strands of her hair as he held her in place for his kiss. His other hand closed over the soft curve of her ass and lifted her higher. He delved deeper and heard her gasp into his mouth, but this was a sigh of pleasure. Her arms went around his neck, clinging to him as tightly as he was holding her. His knees weakened as all the blood in his body rushed to his aching cock, and he staggered.

The awkward movement brought him to his senses, and he reluctantly lifted his head. Her face was flushed, her eyes heavy, and her mouth red and swollen. He thought perhaps he should feel remorse, but all he felt was satisfaction at her obvious pleasure.

"I... am sorry." He forced himself to apologize anyway, but he knew he sounded less than sincere.

"Why? I'm the one who kissed you." Her flush deepened, but she gazed at him steadily.

"I believe I took it somewhat further than you intended."

Her lips curved in a sultry smile. "I didn't expect it to happen, but I certainly didn't object."

He appreciated her forgiveness, but his feelings of guilt were finally surfacing. He started to put her back on the bunk, but she kept her arms around his neck.

"What are you doing? I thought we were going to put the mattresses together."

"You still wish to do that?"

"Of course. I trust you."

But could he trust himself? Despite his uncertainty, he gave into temptation. Still holding onto her, he managed to get both mattresses together on the floor, then carefully lowered her onto them. When he started to pull back, she grabbed his hand.

"Please stay with me."

He was helpless to resist the look of entreaty in those big grey eyes. Trying to confine himself to one of the mattresses, he lay down next to her. She immediately curled against his side. His tail wrapped around her waist, and he pulled her closer. A few minutes later, she was asleep again.

Sleep did not come as easily for him. Lingering arousal from their kiss still hummed through his veins, enhanced by her soft body and sweet scent. But despite his aching cock, and his uncertainty about the future, there was nowhere else he would rather be.

CHAPTER TEN

When Claire woke the second time, Arcosta was in the exact same position he had been when she went to sleep, but his tail was wrapped around her waist. She found she didn't mind that at all. It was already a familiar, comforting weight.

Her legs still ached, but despite that, she was filled with happiness. The children were free from Dr. Pagalan, and so was she. When Arcosta had taken Neera and Juni away, everything had seemed so bleak. The future looked so much brighter today. Not that it would be easy, of course. She still had to make sure she could keep the twins and find a way to support the three of them. But she wasn't afraid of hard work—she would find a way.

And then there was Arcosta. She still couldn't believe that she had kissed him, or that the attraction between them had flared so rapidly. When Sarat had attempted to kiss her, she hadn't felt the slightest desire to respond. With Arcosta, she suspected that if he hadn't brought things to a halt, she wouldn't have pushed him away.

HONEY PHILLIPS & BEX MCLYNN

Under other circumstances, she might have been embarrassed, but instead she felt almost smug. There was something oddly freeing about being the one to choose. She was attracted to him, and it was more than just his impressive body—or even the fact that he had rescued them. It was his patience, his kindness. The way he treated the children—and the way he treated her, as if she was precious. She wanted to get to know him better, and now she would have the opportunity.

And the way he responded to her—so urgently—made her feel like a desirable woman for the first time in over a year. Or perhaps even longer. Before she and Evan had decided to have a child, their sex life had settled into an increasingly infrequent routine. Even when they were first together, it had been comfortable rather than passionate. Those encounters had been like the flicker of a candle compared to the raging wildfire of her response to Arcosta.

She ran her fingers thoughtfully along his tail, intrigued by the pattern of small raised nubs. As far as she could tell, that intriguing texture covered his entire body. Did that include his cock? What would they feel like inside her, she wondered with a flare of excitement.

"Kimati, you are testing my control."

A big hand clamped down over hers, and she looked up to see Arcosta wide awake and watching her from those dark mysterious eyes.

"Am I hurting you?"

"Hurt is not the correct term."

He shifted a little as he spoke, and she felt the rigid bar of his cock brush against her ass. *Oh.* The same impulse that had led her to kiss him last night reappeared, and before she could second-guess herself, she squeezed the thick length of his tail. He groaned, and his spicy scent seemed to increase. Satisfaction filled her, but she gave him an innocent look.

"Are you sure I'm not hurting you?"

"I suspect you know quite well that you are not." He smiled down at her, and her heart gave an odd little skip. *Slow down*, she told herself. Reveling in her reawakened interest was one thing, but getting her heart involved was something else.

"What did you call me? Kimati?" she asked, deliberately changing the subject. "You said it last night as well."

The skin across his cheeks seemed to darken, but he didn't look away from her.

"It is a word in the ancient tongue. It means precious."

Her heart fluttered again. So much for changing the subject. She dragged her eyes away from the dark gaze that promised so much, and began to sit up. Her calves immediately started to cramp. She winced, and his expression turned to concern as his arm slid around her waist to support her.

"What is wrong?"

"Nothing that time won't cure. I think last night was a little too much exercise after three months in one room."

"I am sorry I could not come up with a better plan."

"Don't be sorry. You got us out of there, and that's all that matters. I would rather have cramps for the rest of my life than have stayed there." At his horrified look, she quickly added, "But they won't last anywhere near that long. Maybe a shower will help."

"I have a better idea."

Before she could ask, he had placed one of the mattresses back on the lower bunk and lifted her onto it. Lukat gave an outraged squeak when the movement dislodged him. Arcosta laughed and handed him to Claire.

"I do not think he believes it is time to awaken."

She settled the small animal in her lap, stroking his soft pink fur as she watched Arcosta retrieve a large circular container.

"What's that?"

"A tub so you can soak your feet. It should help to relieve the soreness." He gave it a dissatisfied look. "I am sorry that I could not create a larger one."

"This will be perfect," she told him firmly.

He smiled at her and went to fill it with hot water. Unfortunately, the bathroom was so tiny that he ended up soaking himself in the process. As he returned to place the tub at her feet, her eyes traveled down over the wet shirt, now clinging even more tightly to those impressive muscles.

"You should take off your shirt," she said, trying to keep her face innocent. "Give it a chance to dry."

From the look he gave her, she wasn't quite sure she had succeeded, but after a brief pause, he pulled the wet shirt over his head. *Oh my.* No matter how tightly it had clung to him, it wasn't the same as seeing all that bare, naked flesh.

She was still staring at him when he grasped her feet in his big, warm hands and lifted them into the water. She hissed as the hot water covered her feet, but then it settled into a soothing warmth. His hands lingered on her ankles, and she remembered the way he had kneaded her aching muscles the previous night.

"It might help if you rubbed my legs."

She didn't have to ask twice. He began kneading her calves, his strong hands working out the lingering aches, starting at her ankles and moving slowly up to her knees. The ugly hospital gown was halfway up her thighs, and she was suddenly extremely conscious of how close his hands were to her naked pussy. He was so close, his muscles flexing as he worked her legs, and a different ache started between her thighs. His thin nostrils flared, and his hands stilled as his gaze traveled up to where her nipples thrust against the thin cloth and then to her flushed face.

"You are aroused."

"Well, yes. You're touching me."

"My touch arouses you?" He actually looked shocked.

"I thought that was pretty obvious after I kissed you last night."

"I thought I was the one who kissed you." A slow smile crossed his face as he bent closer. "I do not wish to take advantage of you."

"What if I want to take advantage of you?" she whispered as she leaned forward to meet him.

Their lips touched, and just that one simple connection sent flames licking through her system. His hands tightened on her thighs as he drew back the barest fraction of an inch.

"I am an honorable male," he said, but it sounded as if he was speaking to himself rather than to her.

"I know you are. Does that mean you can't kiss me?"

He groaned, and then his mouth was back over hers, as hot and hungry as it had been the night before. His arm came around her waist to pull her closer, and she was vaguely aware of Lukat giving another outraged squeak and scurrying away, but all that mattered was kissing him.

Those big hands parted her thighs, and she jumped as his thumbs slid through the waiting dampness. He plucked at her nipple, the sudden tug making her back arch before she realized that both his hands were occupied. She pulled away long enough to look down and see that his tail was curved around her breast, squeezing the aching peak. But then he growled and covered her mouth with his own again. He tugged her legs further apart, and a thick digit slowly circled her entrance. She tried to push against that tantalizing touch... and a knock sounded at the door.

They both froze, and then Arcosta had her gown pulled

down and was on his feet before she even realized that he was moving.

"Yes?" he asked, his voice strained.

"I want to see Claire."

In spite of the unfulfilled ache between her legs, she smiled at the sound of Beni's demand. Arcosta returned the smile somewhat ruefully, and opened the door. Both twins were standing there with Neera close behind them, a knowing look on her face.

Beni flew across the room and climbed into her lap. Juni stopped to pick up Lukat, then joined him.

"We're hungry," Beni announced.

Arcosta looked appalled.

"I will return with food immediately." He looked at his soaked shirt, then shrugged and left the room, still shirtless.

"I see you took my advice about having fun," Neera teased, her tail swishing as she came and sat down next to her.

Claire blushed and tore her eyes away from Arcosta's retreating figure.

"He got wet filling up my tub," she said with as much dignity as possible.

"If you say so." Neera gave the other mattress, still on the floor, a meaningful look, but Claire ignored her and changed the subject.

"Did you sleep well?"

Neera nodded and stretched gracefully. The girl looked as fresh and energetic as if the frantic race to escape had never occurred.

"I can't believe we're actually free. And that my cousin sent Arcosta for me—for us."

"Do you think he'll mind that there's four of us now?"

"Not at all." The girl put her hand on Claire's arm. "And

don't worry. I told you that his mate was human. She'll make sure that he provides for you."

A growl filled the cabin, and everyone except Juni jumped as Arcosta stalked back in.

"You do not need another male. I will provide for you."

CHAPTER ELEVEN

Arcosta knew he was overreacting, especially when Claire gave him a startled look, but he couldn't help himself. The idea that another male, especially a former pirate like Rafalo, would assume responsibility for Claire and the children went against every instinct he had.

They are mine.

Not that he had much to offer them, he remembered belatedly. His tiny room was no place for family. But perhaps he could use the reward that Rafalo had offered and obtain larger rooms. But the space station itself was not an ideal environment, and he decided he would have to start looking for other employment.

In the meantime, Claire was still staring at him in astonishment, and he forced himself to calm down.

"I took you from the lab. You are my responsibility," he said, trying to sound less aggressive.

Her shoulders straightened as she glared at him. "And I am a fully grown adult. I am quite capable of being responsible for myself and the children."

As he tried to think of a better way to explain, he remembered why he had returned so quickly.

"Udasi has prepared a meal for us."

Beni hopped up immediately, tugging Juni along with him.

Claire was still frowning, but she started to lift her feet out of the tub. As Neera led the children out of the room, he kneeled in front of Claire and put his hand on her arm.

"I did not mean to offend you, kimati. But this is a dangerous world."

"And you think I don't know that?" she snapped, then her body softened and she patted his hand. "I'm sorry. I know you're trying to be helpful, but I've learned I have to take care of myself."

"What can I do to help?"

Apparently, that was the right thing to say. Her face relaxed, and she smiled up at him.

"Teach me more about this world." She hesitated, and he wrapped his tail around her waist. "One of the assistants at the lab brought the twins a learning game. I know it was designed for children, but I was using it to teach myself the written language as well. Do you think there's anything like that on board?"

He spared a regretful thought for his data tablet, left in his cabin on the impounded ship.

"I am not sure, but Udasi has a small library. He may have something. But if we want to keep him in a good mood, we had best join him for the meal."

"Thank you, once again," she said softly and leaned forward to press her lips against his cheek. It was no more than a glancing touch, but it spread warmth throughout his body. He would render her all the assistance of which he was capable so that she might learn, but he silently vowed that he would still do everything in his power to protect her and the children.

"How do your legs feel? Do you want me to carry you?"

"Better, actually. You have a magic touch."

His cock jerked at her teasing look, and he remembered what they had been doing before the children arrived. His tail slid down to her thigh, but she was already lifting her feet out of the water.

"My feet feel better too, but I don't fancy putting the flip-flops back on. Is it okay if I go barefoot?"

"You may go entirely bare if you wish, kimati."

Her gaze flew to his, and that tantalizing little tongue wet her lips.

"I don't think the children would understand," she said, her voice breathless. "And Neera would understand all too well."

"Then perhaps we should join them dressed as we are."

"Food's getting cold." Udasi scowled at them as Arcosta led Claire into the small dining area.

Juni looked up and smiled, but Beni kept his eyes on his plate, eagerly devouring his food. The little girl seemed more interested in finding tidbits for Lukat.

"I'm sorry we're late." Claire gave the old male a sweet smile, and his cheeks actually colored before he ducked his head.

"Claire, this is Udasi. He knows everything there is to know about this route."

"I'm glad we're in such safe hands."

"Just common sense," Udasi muttered, but he looked pleased as he waved them to the table.

"This is so good," Beni said enthusiastically, and a look of distress crossed Claire's face.

"What's wrong, kimati?" He kept his voice low enough for the children not to hear.

"They never had anything but meal packs at the lab. They have missed so much."

"We will do our best to make up for that." His tail curved around her hand and she squeezed it in response. Delighted that she hadn't objected to him using the word *we*, he did his best to ignore the arousing touch. "Now have some food. Udasi is an excellent cook."

She took a bite and hummed appreciatively. Once again, Udasi looked pleased even though he shrugged casually. Arcosta suspected she rose even further in the old male's estimation when she insisted on helping him clean up afterwards. The others helped as well, and then Udasi invited them all to the control room.

"Who's been driving?" Claire asked as she looked at the empty chair.

Udasi cackled. "Automated control. Works well enough, unless there are problems. There are always problems."

She looked at the row of huge vehicles trundling along in front of them.

"Is that why you travel like this?"

"Yeah. Plus, used to be a lot of bandits." Udasi peered at her from beneath bushy orange brows. "Still are."

Her eyes widened, and she looked back at him uncertainly.

"It is also because of the climate." He pointed at the heavy clouds looming over them. "The geomagnetic field generated by the balena ore creates these clouds. As a result, this area suffers from frequent storms. The convoy provides protection and helps make sure no one goes off course."

"Are we in danger?"

"I told you Udasi has years of experience with this route and these conditions." To his relief, she didn't press the matter. There was always danger, but he did not want her worrying.

Both children huddled silently against her as they stared out at the wide valley through which they were traveling. Dark sand streaked with the characteristic red of the balena spread across the floor of the valley, before rising in rocky slopes on either side. Of course, they had never experienced anything like it before—this expanse of open horizon. He kept forgetting that they had spent their lives in Dr. Pagalan's clutches. They hadn't seemed as overwhelmed last night, but perhaps the late hour and the surrounding darkness had helped to curb that response.

Beni's lips trembled, and he reached down and scooped up the boy.

"I have an idea."

Claire took Juni's hand, then Neera shrugged and followed. After a short stop at the storage room, he led them down to the almost empty cargo hold. He wound rubber strips together to form a crude ball and used a piece of pipe as a makeshift staff. Attempting to hit the ball with the staff was an early warrior training technique—designed to improve hand and eye coordination—and it was one of his earliest memories.

The rules were soon forgotten as the exercise devolved into a game of chase, but the hold rang with childish laughter and he was content.

Claire came to join him where he leaned against the wall watching the twins.

"This was a brilliant idea. I think they feel much more comfortable here. I just hope that they don't have lasting problems as a result of spending their early years in the lab."

"They will be fine," he said firmly. "We will slowly introduce them to new experiences."

"We?"

"Unless you wish to take them away from me."

Which he would protest with every breath in his body.

"No. No, I wouldn't do that."

"Good." As they focused on the children again, he added. "That is happening on Ciresia as well."

"What is?"

"Children are being artificially created and raised in a lab. Although not under such limited conditions."

"That's terrible! Why?"

"The Red Death took all of our females. And we were always told that a Cire male could only truly mate with a Cire female. The artificial wombs are an attempt to find a way to keep our race from dying out."

"And is that true? About only mating with a Cire female?"

"No." He wanted to add more, to tell her that he was quite sure that she was his mate, but their future was so uncertain. What if she thought she had no choice but to agree?

Juni wandered over, Lukat nestled in his carrier again, and held up her arms. He picked her up, tucking her warm little body against his chest as they watched Beni and Neera play. But even Beni's energy eventually faded and he came to join them.

"Time for a rest," Claire announced, and he carried both twins back to their cabin.

Claire started telling them a story, and they were asleep long before it ended. As they quietly left the cabin, she gave her garment a rueful look.

"I don't suppose there were any clothes in that storage room?"

"I've never worn an outfit for so long," Neera agreed.

"There may have been a few items that were left behind. I will look."

He managed to find an old shirt and a pair of overalls, but when he handed them to Claire, she wrinkled her nose.

"They smell funny."

Neera took them and gave her a puzzled look. "They seem fine to me. What do you think, Arcosta?"

He stared at Claire, a wild hope making his heart race. A

Cire scent-bonded with his mate, finding the scent of any other female unpleasant. Was it possible that Claire was experiencing the same thing?

"I do not find them offensive, but you do not need them. Perhaps it would be best to wait."

"If you don't want them, I'll take these." Neera grabbed the overalls. "They look much more appropriate for playing games with the twins."

"I don't mind," Claire assured her, sighing. "I guess I'll just keep wearing this. It may not be attractive, but it's practically indestructible. Unfortunately."

The rest of the day flew by. He remembered these trips as being a tedious necessity, Udasi's sardonic conversation the only relief from the boredom. This time, there was always something to do, whether it was helping Beni learn how to hit the ball or holding Juni when she wanted to return to the control room and look out at the desert. Even simply watching Claire as she examined Udasi's books, her expressive face frowning thoughtfully whenever she recognized a word, filled him with contentment.

Their future was still uncertain, so for now he would concentrate on the present.

CHAPTER TWELVE

The sun was sinking towards the horizon, tinting the air an odd coppery color, when Udasi started to slow down. The convoy had reached that night's campsite, the transports pulling off the road and forming a rough semicircle at the base of the rocky hillside. It too had been used many times before, and Arcosta frowned at the bits of debris scattered carelessly against the rocks, some of it half-buried beneath a layer of sand. Had it been this bad when he had traveled this way before? Or had he simply not paid any attention?

"Worthless idiots," Udasi snorted, answering his unspoken question. "They abandon rather than repair. Leave their trash like a bunch of cuhas."

He smiled. The site did remind him of one of the nests of rubbish created by the vermin.

"Does no one try to stop them?"

The old male shook his head. "Nah. Don't care about the planet anymore. Balena oil brought too many credits, too fast, and everyone just wants their piece of it."

He couldn't argue. The refining process that allowed the

extraction of pure balena oil from the ore had generated a great deal of wealth for Maniga. That process had also created the job for which he had been contracted—and for which he had been paid extremely well—but he had seen the effects it had been having on Manigan society. It was one of the reasons he had been so ready to leave when his contract was up.

"Why do you keep driving?"

Udasi shrugged. "Where else would I go? What else would I do?"

He didn't have an answer, but Udasi didn't seem to expect one.

"Better go check on those females," he muttered. "See what they've done to my kitchen."

Arcosta hid his smile as he followed the old male. Claire and Neera had decided to cook the evening meal, refusing any offer of assistance. He wasn't entirely surprised to find the kitchen in complete disarray. An astonishing quantity of pots were piled in the sink, Neera's fur was dusted with flour, and Claire's face was flushed. The children were sitting on one of the counters, something red and sticky covering their mouths and their hands, but they both smiled cheerfully at him.

"What have you done to my kitchen?" Udasi grumbled, looking at the mess.

"We cooked dinner." Claire pulled a dish out of the oven and regarded it doubtfully. The top was uneven, and one side was much darker than the other. "Or at least we tried."

"I am sure it will be delicious," he assured her. "Would you like me to wash the twins' faces?"

"We had jam," Beni announced happily.

"Were you eating it or washing with it?" he asked, and Juni giggled, holding out her arms. Resigning himself to being equally sticky, he picked them both up and whisked them off to the sanitary facility.

When they returned, the dish from the oven was on the table, along with a bowl of wilted vegetables and a basket of small round objects. Udasi was still grumbling as they all sat down to eat.

Despite its appearance, the food turned out to be much better than he expected.

"This is very good."

"I wouldn't go that far," Claire said dryly. "I haven't quite got that oven figured out. Thank goodness Neera was around to help out."

The girl shook her head, but was obviously pleased at the compliment. "I just wish I'd paid more attention when my mother was cooking."

Her mouth suddenly trembled and Claire placed her hand over the girl's.

"You will be back with her before too long, right, Arcosta?"

"I will make sure you get back as quickly as possible," he promised.

Unfortunately, he wasn't sure just how quick that would be. If it turned out that Maniga wasn't one of Tangari's stops, he would have to find a way to get in touch with Rafalo. He might even have to take another contract with the mining company in order to provide for all of them. He hadn't enjoyed the work before, but that was irrelevant. He was more concerned about exposing the females and the children to the rough conditions in the camp.

From the way Claire was looking at him, he was afraid that he hadn't sounded as convincing as he had hoped, but she didn't press the matter. Once the meal was finished, he insisted on helping her clean the kitchen while Neera played another game of chase with the children and Lukat. She wore them out enough that they didn't protest when Claire told them it was time for bed. He carried them to their bunk, then Juni climbed up on his lap with Lukat while Claire told them another story. The children and the gosa fell asleep almost immediately, and as he covered them with a blanket, he looked up to find Claire smiling at him. An almost physical ache of longing struck him.

This. This is what I want.

He had thought that he needed a house, land, a business of his own, but it still would not have been a home. It would not have filled the emptiness inside.

Now, he had no house and no land and no funds, and there was a distinct possibility that the authorities on Maniga were searching for them. But despite that, the emptiness had gone because Claire and the children were with him.

His tail wrapped around her waist, and he started to lead her back to their cabin, determined to show her with his body when he could not yet tell her. Unfortunately, Udasi intercepted him, challenging him to a game of baduka. He hesitated, but Claire had already slipped away from him.

"Go ahead. Neera is going to try helping me learn more of the language from that book you found. I think I'm getting the hang of it, but it helps to have someone go over it with me."

He bit back his frustration and looked over to find Udasi smirking at him, a knowing twinkle in his eyes.

"Come along, boy. Let's see if you've learned anything since you've left."

Despite his disappointment, the evening passed pleasantly. Claire and Neera worked on her schooling while he and Udasi played. He found himself watching her again, happy to see her smiling. Udasi took advantage of his distraction and won the first game, but he won the second.

"Another one?" the old male asked, but Claire had come to join them, leaning against his side as if she belonged there.

"I think it's time for bed," she said softly, and he rose immediately.

"Are you sleeping with the children tonight?" Neera asked innocently as he started to lead Claire out of the room, and he came to an abrupt halt.

"I..."

He gave Claire a helpless look and saw that her cheeks had turned pink. Neera laughed.

"I'm just kidding. I'll watch over them."

"Are you sure?" Claire asked.

"It's fine. But I might challenge Udasi to another game first."

"You?" Udasi actually looked shocked.

Neera sauntered over to him, her tail swishing back and forth.

"Unless you're afraid of being beaten by a female."

Udasi scowled and started setting up the board.

"I wonder if she knows how to play," he said softly to Claire as they left the room.

She laughed. "She does. She was watching the two of you play, and I suspect she's actually pretty good."

Despite his desire for her, his early urgency had faded. There was something deeply satisfying about simply entering their shared room and knowing they would be together—not just tonight, but tomorrow and for as long as he could keep her.

As the door closed behind them, Claire yawned and stretched, then gave him a rueful smile. "There are times when I really envy Neera her youth. I'm still stiff. Maybe I'll fill up the foot tub and pretend I'm taking a real bath. A nice hot one."

Her words triggered something in his memory, and he thought back to his previous journeys. Was this the right camp-site? He was almost positive it was, but he decided to go and check with Udasi first.

"I have a better idea. I will return shortly."

He found Udasi scowling at the baduka board, while Neera did something in the kitchen.

"Did she beat you already?"

"Took me off-guard. Won't happen a second time." Despite the frown on his face, the old male looked impressed.

"Do the waters still run in these hills?" he asked.

Udasi tilted his head. "As far as I know. No one ever uses them anymore."

"What about the other drivers?"

"Newcomers. Doubt they ever heard of them." He snorted. "Never shown much inclination to cleanliness either. Why?"

"I thought perhaps Claire..."

The annoying twinkle returned.

"Not a bad idea. But don't let anyone see."

"I will not," he promised and slipped away just as Neera returned with two mugs of shoko.

He was on his way back to the cabin when he remembered Claire's feet. Swearing under his breath, he made a quick detour to the supply room. When he finally returned, she was sitting on the lower bunk. Her eyes were heavy, but she gave him a teasing smile.

"I was beginning to think you didn't want to sleep with me."

"I always want to be with you," he assured her.

Her eyes flew to his, an unspoken question in them, and he had to remind himself once again that this was not the time.

"But I thought we might do something else before we sleep. Would you like to go outside?"

"I would love to—but Udasi said it wasn't a good idea to let anyone from the other transports know we're here."

"I will make sure that we are not discovered," he promised as he kneeled in front of her and picked up a small foot. "I made these to protect your feet."

The foot coverings were nothing more than rubber strips, padded with more packing material and tied to her feet, but she was as delighted as if he had presented her with jeweled sandals.

"These are perfect! Thank you so much, Arcosta."

She leaned forward and pressed her sweet lips to his. Desire roared through him and for a moment, he was tempted to abandon his plan. But she had seemed so thrilled at the idea of leaving the transport that he sternly ignored his aching cock and rose to his feet, holding out his hand.

"Come with me."

CHAPTER THIRTEEN

C laire's heart thudded with excitement as she followed
Arcosta down the stairs to the exit door. Part of her
excitement was because of the chance to be outside again. She
felt safe in the transport, but it was another confined space,
even if it was much larger than the lab.

But it was more than just the thought of freedom that
thrilled her. She was going to be alone with Arcosta and away
from everyone else.

I wonder if I should seduce him, she thought, then blushed.

The old Claire, the Claire whose life had revolved around
her career and who had never experienced loss, would never
even have considered such a thing. But the new Claire, the
Claire who knew how quickly things could change, didn't want
to waste one minute of the time they had together.

Arcosta opened the door and peered out into the night. She
heard a burst of laughter, but it was coming from the far end of
the camp and there was no one in sight.

"You will have to be quiet. We do not want to attract attention," he warned her, as he quietly lowered the ramp.

"I understand. Udasi told me he didn't trust the other driv-ers." She thought of the old male, hunched in his seat as he trundled back and forth endlessly across the desert. "It seems like a lonely life, especially if he isn't friends with the other drivers. Why do you think he keeps doing it?"

"I asked him the same thing, and he said he did not have anywhere else to go. He has no family." He looked down at her, his face solemn. "I understand what that is like—not to have anyone to care for—and it leaves a male feeling empty."

She thought back to how he had reacted earlier. "But you said you would provide for us."

It wasn't a question, but he nodded. "Of course. You and the children have given me... purpose."

Purpose didn't sound very romantic, but the look in his eyes indicated so much more. Sure she was blushing again, she took his hand.

"So what is it you wanted to show me?"

"Come with me."

He led her quietly down the ramp, then around a rocky outcropping at one end of the camp and up the hillside. The climb was easier than it looked, and aside from dislodging a few small rocks, she made it in silence. The night wind swirled through the rocks, the metallic scent she had noticed before even stronger here, but she enjoyed the feel of the breeze on her skin. Her only regret was that when she looked up at the sky, no stars were visible, only the occasional glimpse of the twin moons through the heavy clouds.

At the top of the hill, a dark opening was framed between two pillar-like formations. She eyed it suspiciously. Surely he didn't intend to go in there? But he tugged gently on her hand and started to lead her into the cave.

"Wait a minute, I can't see in the dark." She frowned up at him. "Can you?"

"Not in total darkness, no. But I do not need a lot of light to be able to see."

"That looks like total darkness to me," she said, pointing to the opening. "Who knows what might be in there waiting for us?"

"The only thing waiting is your surprise." He gently squeezed her hand. "Trust me, kimati."

She did trust him, she realized, and with a soft sigh, she allowed him to lead her into the darkness.

They made one turn, and then another, and she slowly realized that she could make out some of the details of the surrounding rocks. A faint blue glow came from up ahead, growing stronger as they drew closer, and she noticed that the air began to feel warmer.

Stalactites dripped down from overhead, creating elaborate formations. They passed through a maze of matching stalagmites before emerging next to a pool of glowing blue water. Steam wafted gently above the surface.

"Is this a hot spring?" she exclaimed in delight.

"Yes, it is. I thought of it when you said you wished for a hot bath."

"How did you know it was here?"

"It used to be quite common to enjoy the springs when camped at this site, but Udasi says most of the drivers no longer know about it."

She bent down and trailed her fingers through the water. A sparkling blue trail followed the movement. The water was blissfully hot, and she couldn't wait to get in, except...

"I don't have a bathing suit."

"Do you normally wear clothes for bathing?" he asked, his face serious but his eyes smiling.

"Well, no, but..."

His face softened. "Do you wish me to leave you alone, kimati?"

"No," she decided at once, then shook her head at her own inconsistency.

One minute she was thinking about seducing him, the next she was feeling embarrassed at revealing her naked body to him. Without giving herself a chance to second-guess it, she let the cloak fall, then unfastened the gown and let it drop to the ground as well. The expression on his face was everything she could have hoped for. Admiring. Tender. Hungry.

"You are so beautiful, kimati."

She fought back the immediate impulse to contradict him, and smiled instead.

"Can you take off these clever little foot coverings you made?"

He immediately kneeled in front of her, clasping her calf in his big, warm hand as he raised her foot.

"We seem to keep ending up in this position," she murmured.

"I have no objection."

He slipped the makeshift slippers off her feet, then looked up and smiled at her. He was so tall that even kneeling, his head was on the same level as her breasts. If she leaned forward, even the slightest amount, her nipples would brush against his mouth.

"Do your legs ache? Would you like me to rub them again?"

His question decided the matter. Even though she could tell that he was massively erect, he was thinking of her comfort rather than his own needs.

"No," she whispered as she leaned forward. "That's not the part of me that aches."

He opened his mouth as if he were about to ask her the obvious question, but as he did she pressed an aching little peak to his lips. His eyes grew impossibly darker, and then that wonderfully textured tongue swept across her nipple. He groaned, and his hands clamped around her waist as he pulled her closer. She clutched his shoulders, her legs weakening at the pleasure rushing through her body. His spicy scent surrounded her, richer and deeper in the warmth of the cavern. His tail curled around her thigh, then slipped higher. She remembered the tantalizing feel of it from earlier and willingly slid her legs further apart.

Just these minor touches and she was already slick and ready for him. In another life, she might have been embarrassed, but as his tail slid easily through her folds, he growled his approval against her mouth. He pulled her nipple further into the heated depths of his mouth as his fingers repeated the same motion on her other breast. He kept a firm grip on her waist as his tail began probing at the soaked entrance of her pussy.

Oh my God.

As he pressed inside, those wonderful nubs stroked the sensitive inside of her channel and her legs started to shake. Her nails dug into his shoulders as he went deeper, pressing against a spot inside her that literally made her see stars. The cavern seemed to whirl around her as her climax rushed over her with such sudden, shocking intensity that she almost collapsed. But Arcosta would never let her fall.

She clung weakly to him as he finally released her nipple and smiled up at her.

"Did I relieve your ache?"

A choked giggle escaped her lips.

"You certainly did." She shivered happily, the aftershocks from her orgasm still bubbling through her system. "Although that's the kind of ache that needs constant attention."

"I would be happy to assist you whenever you wish."

She had absolutely no doubt that he was sincere, but...

"What about you and your aches?"

"I will survive."

Before she could gather up the courage to suggest an alternative, he lifted her into his arms, then carefully lowered her into the pool of hot water. It was deeper than she expected, the water reaching her nipples as her feet reached the bottom, and slightly effervescent. The hot water bubbled and swirled around her body, and she sighed happily.

"This is wonderful. Thank you for thinking about bringing me here."

"You are most welcome."

He was still standing on the edge of the pool, watching her, and she raised her head.

"Aren't you going to join me?"

"I have no bathing clothes."

He said it so solemnly that it took her a moment to realize that he was teasing her.

She echoed his earlier response. "Do you normally wear clothes for bathing?"

When he shook his head, she laughed. "Then take them off and come and join me."

He didn't wait for a further invitation. As she watched, he stripped the shirt off over his head, his massive shoulders and chest as impressive as they had been earlier. He unfastened his belt, toed off his boots, and then slipped off his pants and his cock sprang free. Her mouth went dry. She knew she was staring, but she couldn't help herself. He was huge—so big she wondered if she could even take him—and, as she suspected, covered with more of those exquisite nubs. Aside from that, he was shaped very similarly to a human male—an extremely large human male. His cock was a long, thick column, with a wide, flat head, and small bulge near the base of his shaft.

His cock jerked at her survey, but he didn't say anything, simply letting her look. When she finally tore her gaze away, he slipped into the water next to her. His tail curved around her waist, pulling her closer, and she didn't resist. Even though she could feel the heated bar of his cock against her stomach, hotter even than the water, and even though desire fizzled through her system like the bubbles in the water, she was content to remain in his arms.

At last he moved away slightly to retrieve a small patch of moss from the edge of the pool.

"What's that?"

"It has cleansing properties. Do you see?"

He wet it, then rubbed it between his fingers to create a pleasant-smelling foam.

"That's great."

She reached for it enthusiastically, but he shook his head. "Please allow me."

Alrighty then. Even though her cheeks were heating again, she nodded.

He washed her with slow, exquisite thoroughness, even going so far as to bend her back over his arm while he massaged the foam through her hair. By the time he was finished, she was spotlessly clean—and more aroused than she had ever been in her life. The constant feel of his big hands on her body, his tail helping to hold her in position, and the frequent brush of that massive cock against her bare skin had left every inch sensitized and ready.

"Arcosta," she whispered.

"Yes, kimati?"

"I ache again."

He immediately lifted her out of the pool and laid her back against the smooth stone. He remained standing in the water, stepping between her legs as he gently pushed them apart. His eyes heated as he traced a careful finger through her folds. Embarrassed by his intense scrutiny, she did her best not to blush.

"You are beautiful here as well, kimati. Pink." His finger circled her entrance. "Delicate." He explored higher and found her clit, brushing it with his thumb. "Sensitive," he added as she cried out. "This pleases you?"

"Yes," she managed to say as he bent forward and slowly licked the sensitive nub. He slid a finger inside, even that one digit stretching her, but it only increased her pleasure.

He began to experiment—licking, sucking, nibbling—using her soft cries and the reactions of her body to learn what she liked. A second thick finger entered her, and he hummed approvingly as she tried to arch into his touch. Her body shook, hovering on the edge of orgasm, but he kept her there, gentling his touch as he stroked slowly in and out. With each shallow stroke, she could feel the texture of his skin scraping against the inside of her channel, firing the sensitive nerve endings. Her clit felt hot and swollen, throbbing against the elusive brush of his tongue.

"Arcosta, please!" she cried.

He thrust his fingers deeper in one hard stroke as he sucked her clit into his mouth, and she exploded. Her climax roared over her like a freight train, temporarily turning her blind and deaf as her body convulsed in long waves of helpless ecstasy.

She was still quivering when he climbed out of the pool and settled down next to her. He smiled, his hand lightly touching her cheek as his tail curved possessively over her leg. He was still erect, enormously so, small golden drops gleaming on the tip of his cock, but he seemed content with her orgasm. But despite the intensity of her climax, she wanted more. She wanted them to experience it together. Reaching over, she tried to pull him closer.

"I want you inside me," she whispered. He hesitated, and her heart skipped a beat. "Do you not want that too?"

"More than anything."

"But?"

"I suspect that once I am inside you, I will knot."

"Knot? What does that mean?"

He took her hand and slid it down his thick shaft to the bulge she had noticed. "This is my knot. Once I'm inside my ma—"

He came to an abrupt halt, and her heart thudded against her ribs. What had he been about to say? His *mate*? She had heard enough of Dr. Pagalan's ramblings to know that a mate bond was very important to some alien species.

"Once I'm inside *you*," he continued at last, and she wasn't quite sure if she was disappointed or relieved. Even though she was overwhelmingly conscious of the attraction between them, the concept of an instantaneous mating bond was so different from her long, drawn-out courtship with Evan.

"My knot will expand and lock us together as you climax and I release my seed."

Now her heart rate was erratic for an entirely different reason. She couldn't even close her hand around his shaft now —how much larger would he be when he expanded?

"Will... will it hurt?"

He looked appalled. "I would never hurt you, kimati."

"Then come to me."

CHAPTER FOURTEEN

Arcosta's heart threatened to beat its way out his chest as Claire raised her arms to him. She was so beautiful, so perfect. Her wet body glistened in the dim glow, an occasional blue sparkle lighting up her pale skin as she moved. He had never wanted anything more, even though he knew once he knotted inside her, the mate bond would lock in place. There would never be another female for him. But wasn't that already true? He didn't need the physical act to know that she would always be his mate.

She shivered, the taut little buds of her nipples tightening, and he abandoned his questions. His female needed him.

He traced a finger across a tempting little peak, and she shivered again.

"I love the way you touch me," she murmured, lifting into his hand.

"And I love to touch you."

He tightened his grip on her nipple, and she moaned, then tugged impatiently on his shoulders.

"Inside me. Now."

His cock jerked, eager to obey, but he refused to rush. He had promised not to hurt her. As he worked her nipples, his tail slipped between her legs. Perfect—she was still hot and slick from her last climax. He probed deeper, and her channel gripped him so tightly that he growled. Hanging on to his control by the barest margin, he slid his tail free and notched his cock at her entrance. The small pearl of her pleasure peeked out from the top of her slit, pink and swollen, and he brushed his thumb against it as he slowly, so slowly, pressed inside.

Her body resisted, but he maintained a steady pressure as he gently circled the small bud and she finally flowered open. He sank in a glorious inch, then two, then paused when he realized her entire body was shaking.

"Are you all right, kimati?"

"Just... I've never... I'm perfect." Her voice trembled, but her brilliant smile reassured him.

As he pressed deeper into the hot, silky embrace of her body, she suddenly cried out, her body tightening around his cock until he couldn't move. The base of his spine tingled, and he was afraid that he would climax, even though he was not yet embedded in her body. But her body finally loosened and he plunged deeper, his way eased by the increased slickness of her channel. He slowed again as she resisted the thickness at the base of his cock, but he stroked her little pleasure pearl until the tight ring softened enough to take him.

As soon as he was fully embedded, his control vanished. Fire raced down his spine as his body thrust helplessly. He heard her cry out as his knot expanded, locking them together as his seed filled her in long, hot pulses. Her channel spasmed around him, almost painfully tight as she milked every drop of seed from his helpless body until he collapsed, drawing her into his arms. He clasped her as tightly as his knot locked their bodies together, and he was filled with utter contentment.

His female—his *mate*—was in his arms, and he would never let her go.

THE AFTERSHOCKS OF CLAIRE'S CLIMAX KEPT RACING through her system as she quivered in Arcosta's arms. He had kept his promise—he hadn't hurt her—but his sheer size and the final shocking stretch of his knot had overwhelmed her system. He filled her completely, and she could still feel his nubs pressing against her sensitive channel. She tried an experimental squeeze, increasing the pressure, then gasped as a mini orgasm washed over her.

"Kimati," he growled in her ear. "If you keep doing that, we will be locked together for a very long time."

"I don't mind," she said breathlessly.

He laughed and kissed her, but seemed content just to hold her.

When his knot finally released and he slipped free of her body, he showed no desire to leave, only pulling her closer to him. She breathed in his comforting, spicy scent, her whole body limp and relaxed. Already half-asleep, she watched the stalactites overhead gleaming in the reflection of the water, the blue tint turning them into magical spires and castles. Evan would never have brought her here. He hated caves.

She didn't even realize that she had spoken aloud, until Arcosta asked, "Who is Evan?"

Oops. This is awkward. She hadn't had a chance to tell him she had been married before, and this was the worst possible time she could have brought it up. But if there was any possible future between them, he needed to know the truth.

"He was my husband," she admitted, trying to keep her voice steady.

He abruptly released her and sat up.

"Husband? Do you mean a mate?" His skin actually paled, the darker striations unusually vivid against the pallor.

"Yes. I'm sorry I didn't tell you before, but things have been rather busy."

He rose to his feet and paced the few steps back and forth across the cavern, his tail lashing.

"I did not realize. I would never have touched you..."

"You don't understand. He died." She sat up as well, concerned about his agitation.

"And you mourn him still."

He seemed to have no doubt about the matter, but Claire was not as sure. She had worked through her grief during that year in Colorado, and now she could remember him fondly. He hadn't been a bad husband—when they were together. But they were both so busy with their careers that togetherness was more the exception than the rule. At least they had managed to coordinate their schedules long enough for her to get pregnant. Her throat threatened to close, and she firmly pushed the memory aside.

"He is a part of my past," she said finally. "I'm more concerned about the future now."

A future she wanted Arcosta to be part of, even though he had made no promises. He still looked uncertain so she held out her hand.

"I'm not betraying his memory, I promise I'm not thinking about him. I'm here with you, and there's nowhere else I would rather be."

The truth of that statement struck her with blinding certainty as he came back to join her. He sat down next to her, his tail immediately curving possessively around her waist. His body certainly didn't seem to share his concerns about her former marriage.

"I am happy to be here with you as well," he said quietly.

Her heart did that odd little flutter again, but she resolutely returned to more physical matters.

"I'm glad, because I have another ache that needs relieving."

She raised his hand to her breast, and his eyes darkened as he stroked his thumb across her nipple.

"Then I shall do my best to assist you."

He bent his head to kiss her, and all thoughts of the past were abandoned in the pleasure of the present.

She fell asleep after the second round of lovemaking, lulled by the warmth of the cave and the satisfaction filling her body, and woke to find him watching her, his eyes warm enough to make her heart flutter again.

"Was I asleep for long?"

"A little while, but I suspect you needed the rest."

"Have you been watching me the whole time?"

"Of course. Such a beautiful sight must be appreciated."

As her cheeks heated, he ran a gentle finger across the scars on her hip.

"You were injured."

"Yes."

"What happened?"

For so long her automatic response had been to refuse to talk about the accident, but looking into Arcosta's dark, patient gaze, she suddenly found her tongue.

"It was a car accident. We were driving home after a doctor's appointment." The sky been heavy and dark, rain beating against the windshield, but she had felt filled with light. "We hit a slick patch of road and Evan lost control." She didn't remember the crash at all. Just waking up in the hospital. "My husband was killed, and I... I lost my child."

"Oh, kimati. I am so sorry."

"When I got out of the hospital, I sold everything and just left my old life behind. I ended up in a small town in the mountains. Somehow it helped to be able to look up and see the stars."

His hand jerked.

"What is it?"

"Nothing important. Is that where you were when you were taken?"

"Yes." She sighed and sat up, her contentment fading as the memories of the past three months surfaced. "The most ironic part of it all was that in an odd way, Dr. Pagalan was trying to give me what I wanted."

"I do not understand."

"You didn't know about his work?"

"No. I was simply sent there by Neera's cousin to retrieve her." He smiled at her. "But I was lucky enough to discover you and the twins as well."

"Thank goodness!" She returned his smile. "What I mean was that Dr. Pagalan is working on extending the fertile years for older females."

"He was trying to get you with child?"

"Artificially, yes." Her gaze focused on the far wall. "I almost wanted him to succeed—except that he would have taken the children and sold them."

"He is a worthless male," he agreed. "Did you say *children*?"

"Yes, part of his research was also to increase multiple births so that a species could repopulate more quickly. From what I understood, the twins were his first success."

"And you..." His hand traced lightly over her stomach.

"He tested me that evening, before you came back, and said it had failed." She did her best to smile. "I suppose I should be glad—who knows what he was using for his experiments?—but it just seemed like my last chance."

He didn't say anything, just stroked her back with a soothing hand. The disappointment of that announcement still stung, but at last she gave him a more genuine smile.

"At least I have the twins." She smiled ruefully. "I guess you could say he gave me a family after all."

"The twins and—" He stopped, sighed, and shook his head. "We can discuss this later. Right now, I want you again before we return."

She wanted to know what he had been about to say—had he intended to include himself in her family?—but he was right. These stolen hours had to come to an end; their family was waiting for them.

Her fingers traced down the ridges of his abdomen to tease at his already stiffening cock.

"Do you ache here?" she whispered.

"Very much so."

"Then I will do my best to relieve it."

Her hand tightened around him, and there was no more talking.

CHAPTER FIFTEEN

The wind had started to pick up when they finally left the caves. Even though it was still dark, Arcosta could see the clouds overhead moving rapidly across the sky. The thick, metallic scent of the balena filled the air.

"Storm coming," he murmured to Claire as they started to pick their way back down the hillside.

"Is that a problem?"

"It should not be. The vehicles are designed to withstand the weather, although we may have to travel more slowly as a result."

But despite his reassuring words, he found himself moving more quickly. An uneasy feeling skated down his spine. As they rounded the last curve of rock, he came to an abrupt halt and she almost ran into his back.

"Why did you stop—"

Her eyes widened as she followed his gaze to the camp— the abandoned camp. All of the vehicles were gone.

"The children! And Neera. Why would Udasi leave us?"

"He wouldn't," he said grimly as he caught the hint of a

different type of metallic scent. *Fuck.* That was blood. "Wait here."

He followed the scent to the abandoned fire. *Fuck.* Udasi's body lay crumpled next to it, his face covered in blood. As he bent down over the old male, he heard Claire gasp behind him.

"Is he—is he dead?"

Udasi's eyes fluttered open as Arcosta reached for his pulse.

"Not yet," the old male muttered, his voice hoarse. "Deserve to be."

"What happened?"

"I was a fool. Saw a bunch of activity around the fire. Came out to find out what was going on." Udasi's voice shook, clearly exhausted. Arcosta wanted to urge him to rest, but he had to know what happened to the children.

"They wanted to leave. Because of the storm. When I objected..."

The old male's voice trailed off again as his eyes closed, but the rest was obvious, and anger roared through Arcosta. They had knocked Udasi out and taken his vehicle, leaving him for dead. The bastards probably expected that any evidence of their actions would be destroyed by the oncoming storm.

Claire clutched his arm. "What about the children and Neera? He said the other drivers couldn't be trusted."

"Remember that they did not know Udasi had passengers. They would not have had any reason to look for them," he said, trying to reassure himself as well as her. "And if they were in a hurry to get going, they wouldn't have stopped to search the vehicle."

It was a reasonable assumption, but it didn't prevent the dread crawling up his spine.

"But they wouldn't know what happened. What if one of them wakes up and—" Claire's eyes filled with tears.

I have to be there before that happens, he thought as the

swirling wind flung tiny grains of sand against his cheek. *Before they reach the mining complex and have time to inspect the vehicle.*

He was a fast runner. On his own, it was just possible that he could catch up with the transports, but he couldn't abandon Claire and Udasi. Another gust of wind swept through the abandoned camp, hard enough to make Claire stagger and send some of the debris flying. A torn piece of fabric fluttered against the rocks, and that gave him an idea.

"Stay with him," he urged Claire.

"But what about—"

"I have an idea. Just wait here."

He could tell that she wanted to demand answers from him, but she only nodded. He paused just long enough to brush a kiss against her mouth, then went off to scavenge.

By the time he found everything he needed and assembled it, the sun had risen but very little light penetrated the increasingly heavy clouds and dust-laden air. He gave the sky an uneasy glance as he returned to Udasi and Claire.

"He hasn't regained consciousness," she said quietly. "I'm worried about him."

"They have a good medical facility at the mines. They will be able to help him," he said, trying to infuse his voice with confidence even though the old male's harsh, shallow breathing worried him as well.

"But how are we going to get there? You can't carry him the whole way," she added as he bent down and carefully picked up Udasi.

The old male felt appallingly fragile in his arms, his body still limp and unresponsive.

"I do not intend to. Come with me."

She followed him silently across to the pieces of debris he had cobbled together. A curved panel from the side of a transport formed a small platform on top of two long metal runners made from discarded crates.

"You made a sled? Are you going to pull him?"

"A little better than that, I hope."

He gently placed Udasi on the platform, then urged Claire to sit down behind him. Once they were both in place, he raised the crude mast and locked it into place.

"Hold on," he warned her, then opened the makeshift sail as he stepped up behind them.

The wind caught it immediately, with a force that threatened to knock him off his feet. For an interminable second, nothing else happened and then the sled started to move, slowly at first, then faster as it overcame the initial resistance.

Claire was clinging to the platform with one hand and Udasi with the other, but she looked up at him, her eyes wide.

"We're sailing."

"That is the idea," he agreed, his attention focused on controlling the sail.

The combination of the ungainly craft and the gusty winds made it difficult to maneuver, but the road traveled by the vehicles was smooth beneath the runners and they gradually picked up speed. Thank Granthar. He suspected they were moving far more quickly than the cumbersome transport vehicles. With any luck, they would reach the mining complex shortly after they arrived.

It wasn't a pleasant trip. Even his arms grew tired from fighting to control the sail. The wind grew steadily stronger, flinging stinging particles of sand and debris at them. Claire didn't complain, although he could see her face growing pale with exhaustion. Despite that, she never let go of Udasi.

The sky grew even darker, and he was just beginning to wonder if they would have to take refuge from the storm when he saw the lights of the mining complex in front of them.

"We are almost there," he yelled over the roar of the wind.

She nodded, her face white and anxious.

The strongest burst of wind he had felt yet grabbed hold of the sail, actually lifting the sled off the ground before the fabric tore and it went tumbling across the ground. He just managed to grab hold of Claire and Udasi, wrapping himself around them before they hit the ground. They landed hard enough to knock the breath out of his lungs, and it took a moment for him to realize that Claire was pushing at his arm.

"It's all right, Arcosta. You can let go of me."

"Never," he said, even as he reluctantly released her.

She flashed him a quick smile before she bent over Udasi's limp body.

"He's still breathing, but he looks even paler."

"We need to get him to the medic and then find his vehicle."

He rose to his feet, once again carrying Udasi. Claire stood as well, but another gust of wind almost knocked her back down. His tail caught her just in time, tugging her against his side as they hurried for the gates to the complex.

The large main gates were closed, but the smaller door opened when he banged on it.

"Where the hell did you come from?" The guard gaped at them.

"Across the desert. This male is injured. He needs a medic as soon as possible."

"I don't understand." The guard frowned at them. "That looks like Udasi, but his vehicle came through just a short time ago."

"It was stolen by other members of the convoy."

The male looked outraged, already raising his communicator to his lips.

"I'll send a team to retrieve it immediately. Do you know where the medical office is located?"

He nodded, even though he wanted to insist on accompanying the team going after the transport. But his friend needed help. Claire also bit her lip, but she didn't protest as they set out again. The tall walls provided more protection from the wind, and he made it to the medical center in a matter of minutes. The medical team rushed the old male away, and he immediately headed back to the door, Claire following him. Her face was pale, and she looked exhausted.

"You should wait here," he told her.

She shook her head, a determined look on her face.

"I have to know if they're all right."

"I understand." He couldn't deny her, but at least he could help. He lifted her into his arms, hoping she couldn't feel how weak he had become, then set off at a run to the transport center.

They arrived just as a couple of guards were marching one of the convoy drivers away from Udasi's vehicle. The guards were rounding up the other drivers as well, but there was no sign of Neera or the children, and his heart thudded against his chest. Claire's hands tightened on his arm, but he could feel them trembling.

"Was there no one else on board?" he asked one of the guards, his voice sounding strange in his ears.

The guard shook his head. "No. Why? Were you expecting anyone?"

They had to be there. They had to be hiding.

Ignoring the guard's question, he kept going. He carried Claire up the ramp, then stopped, not sure where to start looking. Where would they hide?

"In the cargo hold?" Claire suggested, and he realized he had spoken out loud.

As soon as they entered the space, he realized it was hopeless. There was no place to hide.

They looked at each other, and he could see tears sparkling in Claire's eyes, but she refused to let them fall.

"Let's try the cabins."

As they turned back towards the stairs, he heard a faint chittering noise. *Lukat.* His heart beating even faster now, he searched for the gosa. A flash of pink drew his attention to the gosa, peeking out from behind one of the crates, even though he could have sworn that it was flush against the wall. He grabbed Claire's hand and tugged her after him.

"What is it—Lukat!"

At the sound of her exclamation, a small face appeared. Beni. The boy raced across the floor towards them, followed immediately by Juni. The children threw themselves into their arms as Claire burst into tears and he wrapped his tail around all of them.

"Where's Neera?" Claire demanded, just as the older girl appeared, wiggling out of the seemingly impossible space behind the crate.

"I'm here." Tears streamed down her face as well as she grabbed Claire's outstretched hand. "Thank Hebra you found us. Or maybe I should say thank Juni. And Lukat," she added, hiccupping.

"What happened?" he asked.

"Beni woke me up. He said Juni said we had to hide. I didn't know where else to go so we came down here, but I couldn't figure out where to hide until Lukat went behind that crate." Neera dashed away her tears. "The wall curves out and makes a little compartment back there. We just managed to get into it before we heard strange voices. What happened?"

"Udasi was ambushed."

And he hadn't been there to protect him, or the others. The knowledge of his failure washed over him.

Beni tugged on his sleeve. "Juni said you'd come."

"I should have been here."

"But you came," the boy insisted, as Juni joined them.

As usual, she didn't speak, simply holding up her arms to be picked up. His heart still aching, he lifted her into his arms. She put her tiny arms around his neck, then to his utter shock, leaned forward and whispered into his ear.

"Always come."

He looked over at Claire and saw her eyes fill with tears as he hugged Juni tight.

"Yes, little one. I will always come for you."

CHAPTER SIXTEEN

Arcosta reluctantly tore himself away from his once again complete family. They were unlikely to remain that way unless he could find a way off the planet. Fast.

Despite Juni's assurance, his guilt still nagged at him as he walked into the main offices of the mining complex. His mood didn't improve when the current director of the facility turned out to be Dhaka. The stocky Manigan male had been Arcosta's supervisor while he was under contract. He hadn't liked him then, and he liked him even less now that he was reclining in a big chair behind an even bigger desk and smirking at him.

"Arcosta Nar'Taharan. I never expected to see you again."

"I did not expect to return."

"Indeed. Then why are you here?"

"I have had a... change in circumstances." Ignoring the inquisitive look in Dhaka's eyes, he hurried on. "I came to ask if Captain Tangari, of *The Lucky Traveler*, is one of the pilots you use to transport balena oil."

"Captain Tangari?" Dhaka stroked his chin thoughtfully. "I can't say I'm familiar with that name."

Fuck. He'd been hoping for a quick trip off the planet.

"I see. Then would it be possible to send an intersystem message?"

Dhaka's attempt to look regretful failed pitifully. "I am afraid those are quite expensive. Unless you have the funds..."

His voice trailed off as Arcosta shook his head.

"Of course, if you were under contract to us, it would be possible to advance you the necessary credits."

Double fuck. It was the last thing he wanted, but he didn't see any other alternative.

"I might be open to a short-term arrangement."

"Half a year would be the minimum—what with all the training required."

"I am already trained," he said, trying not to growl at the male.

Dhaka shrugged. "Things have changed."

"I will also require larger quarters—at least three rooms."

"Indeed?"

Arcosta didn't like the speculative look in the other male's eyes, but he had to have room for everyone.

"That can be arranged," Dhaka said finally. "Although it will mean a larger portion of your credits will be withheld to cover housing costs."

"As long as it is within the standards set by the Confederated Planets," he said firmly. He wouldn't put it past the sleezy male to charge him an amount equivalent to his contract fee simply for housing.

"Of course. I will have the contract drawn up for your signature. Wonderful to have you back, Arcosta."

Dhaka beamed as he escorted Arcosta to the door of his office. Outside, the young Manigan who served as his assistant was talking into a communicator.

"Yes, of course, Captain Tangari. I will inform the director immediately."

Arcosta had Dhaka up against the wall before he could blink.

"You lying bastard. You do know him."

"I... I can't be expected to remember the names of all the pilots." Dhaka attempted to bluster his way out of the situation.

"I do not believe you." Regretfully, he let the deceitful male drop to the ground. He couldn't waste his time on him. He turned to the wide-eyed assistant instead. "Where is Captain Tangari docked?"

"A-At the third hangar," the young male stuttered.

"Thank you."

As he strode towards the office door, Dhaka's voice followed him.

"Does that mean you won't be taking the contract?"

He reached the third hangar just as Tangari came down the ramp. His look of surprise at seeing Arcosta would have been comical under other circumstances, but he was too anxious to get off the planet to be amused.

"Arcosta! What are you doing here?"

"I took your advice," he said grimly.

"I don't understand, but let's go and have a glass of ale while you tell me all about it. There's an excellent—"

"No time." He took a quick look around to make sure there was no one was close by. "Rafalo offered me the credits all right —in exchange for rescuing his cousin's daughter."

Tangari laughed. "That sounds like the type of heroic task that would appeal to you. But how did you end up here?"

"It's a long story, but the most important thing is that I—*we* —need a way off the planet as soon as possible."

"I should be finished loading within the hour." Tangari

grinned at him. "Is the girl attractive? Have you broken your vow of celibacy?"

"Not with her," he said quickly, all too aware of the speculation on the other male's face. "And she is not the only one who is with me. I am also accompanied by two children and a human female."

Tangari's eyebrows practically reached his mane. "You have acquired quite a collection of companions for such a solitary male. But I don't have a lot of additional sleeping quarters."

"We can sleep on the floor if necessary. Just as long as we can leave here."

"Perhaps one of the females would prefer to share my cabin."

The growl escaped before he could control it, even though he knew his friend was only teasing him. "That will not happen."

Tangari raised his hands in mock surrender. "Whatever you say. Now go and get your little band while I make sure we're ready to leave as soon as I've finished loading."

"I will. And thank you, Tangari. I am very grateful."

"That's what friends are for—even when their friends want to keep all the females for themselves." He laughed at Arcosta's expression and waved him away. "Now go, before you start growling again."

Arcosta shook his head and obeyed.

As soon as he left Tangari, he went to the medical office to check on Udasi. The medic pursed his lips disapprovingly.

"He is already awake and demanding to leave."

That sounded like Udasi. "Does he need to remain here?"

"I would prefer it, but it is not medically necessary. We have sealed his wound, and there does not appear to be any lasting damage." The medic grinned. "I told him his skull was too thick to be damaged by such a minor blow."

"May I see him?"

"Yes, of course. Perhaps you can talk some sense into him." The medic hesitated, then gave him an uncertain look. "My understanding is that when you brought him in, you were accompanied by a female."

He nodded reluctantly.

"You should know that word is already spreading. Be cautious."

"Thank you," he said sincerely. "I hope we will not be here much longer."

"I believe that would be best."

As the medic started to turn away, Arcosta had an idea.

"I know you said that you prefer for Udasi to remain here, but would it be possible for him to accompany us instead?"

"It wouldn't be my first choice, but it would be preferable to having him walk out of here on his own. I can provide you with his recommended care—if you're sure you're willing to take on the responsibility?"

"I am." Udasi had been hurt because of him, but in addition to that, he was a friend and Arcosta did not want to leave him alone. "Assuming that he wishes to come with us, of course."

"Of course. I will begin the paperwork while you talk to him."

His chest ached as he walked into the small hospital room. Udasi looked so small and fragile in the hospital bed. But then his eyes opened and he scowled at Arcosta, his gaze as fierce and intelligent as always.

"Took you long enough."

"I apologize for the delay."

"Yeah, yeah. Now, tell me how I ended up in this damn medical facility."

Udasi grinned delightedly as Arcosta explained his makeshift sand sled.

"Can't wait to give that a try."

"You will do nothing of the kind," he said firmly, then hesitated, trying to decide how to broach the subject. "We are leaving, and I thought perhaps you could come with us."

He had never seen the older male look so shocked.

"Me? Come with you? Why?"

"Because we want you to come." He reached out and took Udasi's hand. "And there is nothing for you here."

"What would I do away from Maniga?"

"I am sure there will be jobs for an experienced driver. Or perhaps you could do something else—like become a cook?"

His last suggestion had been purely based on impulse, remembering how peaceful Udasi looked when he was cooking and how pleased he was—no matter how much he tried to hide it—when people liked his food. To his surprise, Udasi nodded thoughtfully.

"Might be time for a change at that. Have to get off Maniga first."

"I have made the arrangements. My friend Tangari is here, and we will be flying out with him."

Udasi snorted. "That cocky bastard? Still, he seems to know how to fly."

Why hadn't it occurred to him to ask Udasi? Of course the driver would be acquainted with the pilots. He should have come to him instead of going to the director.

"We want to leave as soon as possible. Are you up to it?"

"Hell yeah." Udasi climbed out of bed, completely naked, and headed for the door.

"Perhaps it would be best to get dressed first," he suggested. "I would not want my female to be swayed by the sight of your naked body."

Udasi peered at him from beneath his bushy brows. "Your female?"

"My female," he said firmly.

"Better not keep her waiting then."

As Udasi reached for his clothes, Arcosta smiled. His family seemed to be growing every day.

CHAPTER SEVENTEEN

Claire watched Arcosta depart with a sinking heart. Despite Juni's attempt to comfort him, she could tell that guilt was still eating away at him and she felt just as bad. If it hadn't been for her foolish desire for a bath, they never would have left the transport.

But maybe we would have ended up like Udasi instead, she reminded herself.

She would have liked to go and check on Udasi, but before he left, Arcosta had made her promise that they would remain with the transport.

"But why?"

"This is a tough job on an isolated site. The miners can be... difficult, especially when there is a beautiful—two beautiful females around," he added with an apologetic look at Neera.

Neera had grinned and rolled her eyes, but now she paced back and forth restlessly.

"Do you think we could go outside? Not to visit Udasi or anything, but just to get some air."

The twins gave her an entreating look as well, and she

decided that it should be all right. The guards had taken all of the drivers away when they arrived, and she couldn't think of any reason for anyone else to come to the transport shed.

"I suppose it would be all right. As long as we stay here. Would you like that, Juni?"

The girl smiled and nodded, silent once more. The fact that she had spoken at all gave Claire hope, but she wasn't going to push her.

The four of them trooped eagerly down the ramp into the transport shed, Lukat scampering along ahead of them. Although it had walls on three sides, one end was open. Rather than worsening as they had expected, the storm had died down and now only a few lazy puffs of wind disturbed the hard-packed dirt outside. The twins peered at the wide opening, but they looked curious rather than afraid. Arcosta was right, she decided. They would adjust.

She called them back and, after warning them again not to leave the building, taught them how to play hide and seek. Beni had a tendency to squeak and run whenever she got close, but Juni quickly proved to be excellent at hiding. Unfortunately for her, Lukat gave her away twice by trying to climb into her hiding place. Neera always found everyone who was hiding.

"How are you doing that?" Claire demanded after the third time the girl found her.

Neera laughed and tapped her nose. "Kissats have an exceptional sense of smell. Our hearing is pretty good too. I heard your cloak rustling."

"Just as well it's your turn to hide."

She covered her eyes and counted slowly as the others hid.

"Ready or not—"

Her words came to a halt as she opened her eyes and saw a strange male standing in the open wall.

"Ready, are you? That sounds promising," he said as he sauntered towards her.

Like all Manigan males, he was on the short side, but he was powerfully built and her pulse started to race.

Please stay hidden, she prayed desperately, hoping that Neera would keep the children safe.

"Not for you," she said coolly. "I suggest you leave before my mate returns."

"Your mate? I heard some green monster showed up earlier and set the guards on my friends. They said he had a female with him so I thought I'd see for myself."

"He isn't a monster. He's Cire."

He actually stopped advancing for a moment. "He is, is he? In that case, I might need some backup. Hey, boys!" he yelled. "I found her."

Her heart sank as two more males entered the shed.

"She's kinda old," he added disparagingly. "But better than your hand, right?"

Sweat dampened her palms, but she lifted her chin defiantly. "You think that three of you stand a chance against a Cire warrior?"

One of the new males stopped in his tracks, giving the first one an uneasy glance. "Maybe we should let her go, Balat."

"Don't be stupid. She's probably lying. Even if she isn't, there's three of us and only one of him. I'm ready for some fun."

He grabbed her arm as he spoke, but she remembered a long-ago self-defense class and turned into him, ramming her elbow into his stomach before thrusting her knee into his groin. He howled with outrage, but he let her go. She turned to flee, hoping that if she made it out of the shed someone would come to her aid, but the third male, the one who hadn't spoken, caught hold of her. Balat hobbled towards her, raising his fist, but before he could reach her, an outraged growl echoed through the vast shed.

She caught a brief glimpse of Arcosta, and then he moved with that lightning speed she had seen once before, tearing her captor away from her. He disposed of him and Balat so quickly that she was still blinking when Udasi slammed a cane down on her final attacker's head as he tried to flee. Then Arcosta was there, running his hands frantically over her body.

"Are you all tight, kimati? Did they damage you?"

"No, you made it in time." She smiled up at him, tears threatening, but then Neera and the twins came racing towards her.

"Thank Hebra you're all right." Neera hugged her. "I didn't know what to do."

"You did the right thing. You kept the twins safe."

Beni was clinging to one leg and Juni the other, and she kneeled down and hugged them too. She smiled up at Arcosta, but he was looking unusually grim.

"We are leaving," he announced. "Now."

She and Neera exchanged a quick glance, but neither one of them argued. Before she could pick up the twins, Arcosta picked them up, wrapped his tail around her waist and set off. Neera stayed next to Udasi as he hobbled along behind them.

"Are you all right?" she called over her shoulder.

'Never better," he said cheerfully, even though a huge bandage covered half his head and he was leaning heavily on the cane.

"Thank you for coming to my rescue."

Did Arcosta growl again? She wasn't quite sure, but when she looked up, Juni was patting his face with a tiny blue hand. Hmm. As soon as they were away from here, she needed to know what was going on in his head.

A Kissat male met them outside an odd-looking ship with a

narrow top and a much larger base. He looked from her to Arcosta as Arcosta introduced them, then grinned.

"Ah, I see. A jewel amongst—" He broke off abruptly as he spotted Neera behind them, keeping a watchful eye on Udasi. "Holy Hebra."

Neera looked up as he spoke, and their eyes met. The Kissat couldn't blush because of their fur, but Claire watched in fascination as Neera's tail curled. The two were still staring at each other when Arcosta growled.

"Claire was just attacked. We need to leave immediately."

"Yes, of course." Tangari seem to recover his composure, sweeping her an elaborate bow even though his eyes kept returning to Neera. "Welcome to my humble ship, ladies. You will be safe here."

Arcosta's scowl deepened, but he didn't respond as they followed Tangari onto the ship. The majority of the ship seemed to consist of the rather bulbous cargo hold, but he bypassed that and led them directly to the bridge.

"Perhaps it will make you feel more comfortable to watch us depart."

The twins' eyes were wide with excitement, and Arcosta placed them in the chair next to Tangari where they could see everything. A quick word over his communicator, and then Tangari lifted the ship into the air, climbing so smoothly that she could barely even tell that they were moving.

As soon as they made it through the thick clouds, Arcosta turned to her, his features still taut.

"I need to speak to you. Privately."

"Next level down, first door on the right," Tangari said, looking amused.

Arcosta immediately lifted her into his arms and left the bridge. She wanted to protest, but he looked so tense that she decided to wait and see what he had to say.

The door Tangari had indicated opened into a small cabin. She just had time to notice that it was far nicer than any of their previous accommodations, complete with paneled walls and an actual bed, before Arcosta put her down and started pacing a few steps back and forth across the room.

"What is it? What's the matter?" Her pulse started to race. Had he decided that she—they—were too much trouble? "I'm sorry we didn't stay inside the transport."

"What happened was not your fault. It was mine."

"How can you say that?"

"I call myself an honorable male, but I cannot even prevent my mate from being attacked."

Her heart skipped a beat.

"You called me your mate," she whispered.

"Of course you are my mate," he said impatiently, still pacing. "There will never be another female for me."

"You've never said it to me before."

"How could I?" He finally stopped moving and returned to her, taking her hands in his. "I have so little to offer you, kimati. I thought I could at least protect you and the children, but I failed at that."

"You did not fail," she said indignantly as tears filled her eyes. "You got us here in time to find the children, and you came back to the shed before anything happened. Even if you hadn't, I would never blame you. I know you will always try to protect us. I know you will always come."

"Do you mean that?" He was studying her face, but his tail had already encircled her waist.

"Of course I do." A tear slipped free as she smiled at him. "I love you, Arcosta."

He staggered—her big, strong mate actually staggered—and she took advantage of his momentary weakness to push him down on the bed.

"You love me?" he repeated as she kneeled down next to him.

"Of course I do. But..."

His body tensed as she hesitated.

"But you know it's a package deal, right? I mean that the twins come with me as well," she added when he looked confused.

"Where else would they be but with us?"

He still looked adorably confused, and she bent down to kiss him. He groaned as their lips touched and pulled her down at his arms, kissing her so thoroughly that she was shaking by the time their mouths parted.

"We should probably return to them," he said reluctantly.

"You did snatch me away in a bit of a hurry."

"I just kept thinking of that male's hands on your flesh. I love you so much, Claire. I cannot stand to think of anything happening to you."

Happiness bubbled through her veins, and even though she knew he was right, that they should return to the others, she wasn't quite ready to let him go. She unfastened his belt, freeing his already erect shaft.

"Kimati, as much..."

His words disappeared in a strangled gasp as she bent over and licked the tip of his cock.

CHAPTER EIGHTEEN

"What are you doing?" Arcosta asked, unable to hide his shock.

Claire gave him an innocent look. "You don't know?"

He did, of course, but the act had been forbidden on Cire before he left and he had never been tempted to experience it since then. He'd never really understood the appeal, but when Claire looked up at him with those big grey eyes and swiped her smooth little tongue across the head of his cock, he almost exploded.

"I've never..."

"Good."

She hummed with pleasure, the vibration sending another shock of excitement through his cock. Then her hot little mouth closed over his tip, and he had to clench his fists in the sheets to prevent himself from thrusting deeper. She couldn't take much of him, her mouth already stretched wide, but she seemed determined to try, gradually working her way down his cock as she licked and sucked the aching flesh. He just touched her throat when she swallowed around him, and he could no longer remain in control. He exploded with a hoarse cry, hot liquid pulsing out of him as she swallowed again and again, drinking him down.

His knees still felt weak when she finally raised her head and smiled at him.

"That was amazing," he gasped.

She hummed again, still smiling, but then she looked at his cock.

"You're still hard."

"I can only truly climax inside my mate."

"That wasn't a climax? You could have fooled me."

"For a Cire, a true climax requires that we knot inside our mate." He had also been told that knotting was required in order to fertilize his seed, but with no more Cire females, it didn't seem relevant.

"Wait a minute. You said 'inside your mate,' but you knotted inside me in the caverns."

"I did."

"You knew then?"

"Of course."

She grabbed a pillow from the head of the bed and smacked him with it.

"Why didn't you tell me?" Her face was flushed, her eyes fierce.

"I did not want to take advantage of you."

His answer sounded weak, even to him, and she rolled her eyes the same way Neera did as she started to climb out of bed.

"You are angry?"

She sighed. "Not angry exactly. But I was starting to feel the same way, and it would have been nice to know that we were on the same page."

He didn't quite understand the idiom, but he recognized the underlying sentiment. His mate needed to know that he loved her. He should have told her then, but since it was too late for that, he would make it up to her now. He grabbed her hand and pulled her back down on the bed, then covered her with his body.

"What are you doing?"

"Proving to my mate how much I love her."

His cock nudged her entrance. Apparently, she had enjoyed taking him in her mouth because she was already slippery and ready for him. *Good.* He pushed inside, working his way into her narrow channel until he was completely embedded.

"This may take a while," he warned.

She laughed, and her tight little cunt squeezed his cock, sending ripples of pleasure down his spine.

"Are you sure about that?"

He forced his body under control, determined to pleasure her as thoroughly as possible. He grasped her hips in one hand, pulling her even deeper onto his cock, then held her there as his tail swept slowly back and forth across her little pleasure button until she gasped and he felt her clenching around him.

"That is one."

Her face was dazed with pleasure, but she managed to give him a challenging look.

"Can you manage two?"

"Can you?"

He slowly withdrew his cock, then entered her again just as slowly, paying particular attention to the places that made her breath catch as he continued the rhythm, rocking her over into her second climax. Apparently, she liked slow. Of course, she also liked fast. Number three came as his control started to slip, and he plunged hard and fast into the silken fist of her body.

When her shudders finally subsided, she was limp and helpless in his arms.

"I think perhaps one more," he murmured, and her eyes flew open.

"I'm not sure I can move."

"That is not a requirement."

He turned her over on her stomach, admiring the smooth lines of her body as he lifted her hips in his hands and slid inside once more. His tail wrapped around the subtle curve of her ass and began to probe delicately at the little pink star between her cheeks.

"Arcosta," she gasped.

"Shh, kimati. You are not moving, remember?"

But as his tail slowly entered that hot little haven, she did move, slowly at first, then faster, thrusting back against him as her fourth climax swept over her. His own control vanished completely, overcome with the pleasure of being joined so intimately. His seed erupted in long, almost painful pulses as his knot expanded and locked them together, and he heard her cry out once more.

He collapsed onto the bed, careful to avoid putting his weight on her, and held her close.

"Mmm." Her eyes were still closed as she entwined her fingers with his. "I like this part."

"I thought you liked all of it."

She giggled, sending a delightful reverberation through their joined bodies. "You know I did. But being locked together like this feels special."

"I agree. I believe this is why a Cire can only knot inside his mate—she is the only one with whom he wants to share this closeness."

They both relaxed into a contented silence until his knot finally released and his cock slipped free. He left her long enough to retrieve a cleansing cloth and gently wipe her swollen folds.

"We should talk to the twins," Claire said as she sat up. Her face was still flushed, her hair in wild disarray, but she glowed with satisfaction.

"What do you mean?"

"I mean let them know that we're together—all of us—as a family. That we're their family."

He rather suspected that the twins already knew, but he nodded. He liked the idea of openly claiming them as his. With his tail firmly around her waist, they went in search of the children. They found everyone in the small lounge.

Neera was playing some type of card game with the twins while Tangari watched her like a lovesick adolescent. From the way Neera kept glancing at him, her tail twitching, she was quite aware of his scrutiny. Udasi scowled furiously at Tangari, but the other male ignored him.

Neera smiled at them as they entered. "Still having fun?"

Claire's cheeks turned pink, but a smile hovered on her mouth. "Definitely. We're mated."

"Well, yeah." The girl rolled her eyes. "I knew that the moment Arcosta came back with you."

"Apparently, I'm the last to know." Claire shook her head, still smiling, then tugged him down on the couch next to the twins. "Beni and Juni, we want to talk to you for a minute."

Both children looked up at her expectantly.

"We want to make sure you know that Arcosta and I are together and you are—"

She didn't get a chance to finish. Juni flung herself into Claire's arms, and he clearly heard her say, "Mama."

Beni tugged on his leg, his small face anxious. "Juni says you're our papa now. Is that right?"

"Yes, it is," he said solemnly.

"Forever and always?"

His chest ached. "Yes. That's what family means."

Beni gave a huge sigh, a brilliant smile appearing on his face. "It's about time."

He laughed and hugged his son, and then a minute later Juni was there too. She kissed him, and whispered to him as well. "Papa."

The rest of the day passed in a blaze of happiness, even though it consisted of the mundane tasks of life on board a ship. Udasi took over the galley while Neera and Claire rummaged through Tangari's small collection of books. The twins were everywhere, Beni effervescent with happiness. Juni was much quieter, but several times she climbed up on his lap and wrapped her tiny arms around his neck. His heart melted every time.

He and Tangari discussed their route and decided to head directly to Rafalo's station. Tangari would resume his delivery schedule afterwards. He showed his appreciation by soundly defeating his friend in two out of three training matches.

The sleeping arrangements were a matter of some debate since Tangari's ship wasn't designed for this many passengers, and he and Claire were occupying the only guest cabin. His friend gallantly offered Neera the captain's cabin, but she refused, preferring to bunk with the twins in the small crew cabin. He saw Claire breathe a sigh of relief, then shoot him a teasing glance, and he suspected she had been afraid the two would end up sharing. Udasi opted for the couch in the lounge area, over everyone's objections, grumpily telling them that he was old enough to make his own decisions. Despite his protests, the old male seemed happy with his decision to join them.

And underneath it all was the knowledge that Claire had accepted him.

His body hummed with desire as he escorted her back to their cabin that evening, already anticipating a repeat of their earlier encounter. He opened the door and a small pink head popped up from the center of the bed, quickly followed by a second, and then a furry little nose.

"What are you doing here?" Claire asked. "Is something wrong? Are you scared?"

"No." Beni grinned at her. "Juni thought we should be together tonight."

Juni nodded solemnly. "Together."

If his daughter thought it was important, he wasn't going to argue. He looked over at Claire and saw her shoulders shaking with silent laughter.

"The joys of parenthood," she said at last.

And even though his body ached with frustrated desire as he climbed in on one side of the twins while Claire took the other side, he agreed. He had his family at last.

CHAPTER NINETEEN

"That's the space station?" Claire asked, her nerves humming now that their destination was in sight.

The trip had been almost like a honeymoon—especially since the twins had not repeated their insistence on joining them in bed. Well, perhaps a family vacation would be more accurate. The twins seemed to grow surer of themselves every day, especially Beni, who followed Tangari around like a little shadow. Claire suspected it severely hampered Tangari's attempts to flirt with Neera—and vice versa—but perhaps that was just as well. The two Kissats were obviously falling in love, but there was no need to rush things. Even though Arcosta had assured her that Tangari was a good male, she still worried about the younger girl.

Udasi had continued to insist on cooking, although he begrudgingly let her help occasionally, and Juni liked to sit quietly in the kitchen watching him. She hadn't spoken again, but Claire was determined not to push her.

Her own time had been spent practicing her language skills, playing with the children, and sneaking off with her mate at every opportunity. Their desire for each other only seemed to increase. A little shiver of pleasure went through her as she remembered their encounters earlier that day. He had pulled her into their cabin, lifted her dress, and used his mouth to bring her to a fast, intense climax before kissing her and going off to train with Tangari while her legs were still shaking. She had returned the favor a few hours later. For someone who claimed that he could only truly climax inside her, his reaction to her mouth was most gratifying, she thought smugly.

But now all of that was coming to an end as they reached Rafalo's station.

She had expected some sort of long, irregular structure, but instead, this was more like a small moon floating in space. A very dirty moon, she realized as they drew closer and she could see that the outside was stained and pitted, even dented in some places. A sigh escaped before she could hold it back.

"What is wrong, kimati?" Arcosta asked softly.

"Nothing."

To her shock, his tail slipped down from around her waist and lightly smacked her butt. The unexpected sting was also unexpectedly arousing, but she ignored that and frowned up at him.

"Why did you do that?"

"Because you are not telling the truth."

"What makes you think that?"

"Your scent changes." His tail curled back around her waist as he smiled down at her.

"So you will always be able to tell if I'm not being truthful? That doesn't seem fair when I won't know that about you."

"I would never lie to you, kimati."

"I believe that, but I also think that sometimes you do not tell me everything."

"Only in an attempt to protect you," he admitted. "But you

are correct. There should be no secrets between mates. Now tell me why you sighed."

"It's not that I'm not grateful to be here. I'm so relieved to be out of the lab and away from Dr. Pagalan."

"But?"

"It's just another confined space. No matter how large it is," she added as they drew closer and she realized the sheer size of the station. "I miss being outside."

"I agree that it is not ideal." He hesitated, then added, "The station is very busy. There are always people coming and going, and they are not usually the nicest people. My room is very small and I will have to get an advance on my salary to arrange for a larger one."

She didn't try to hide her initial dismay—she had asked for the truth, after all—but she raised her chin.

"Thank you for telling me. We'll just have to work together to make it a good home for the children."

"I have no doubt that they will adapt, but I agree, it is not what I would have wished for them."

"The people who you are with are more important than your surroundings," she said firmly. "We will give them love, and that is the most important thing of all."

"Yes, kimati," he agreed as the ship came to a landing.

"Now what do we do?"

"Tangari sent a message once we were in transmission range. Rafalo asked us to dock here, so I expect him momentarily."

Tangari didn't look thrilled by the prospect, and Claire couldn't blame him. From everything Neera had said, her cousin was very protective, and she wasn't sure that he would be happy at her interest in the older captain. Neera's face was a curious mixture of defiance and longing. Claire knew the girl had wanted to return home, but she also suspected she was concerned about any interference in her relationship with Tangari.

"We should meet him as well," Arcosta told her. "I would like to introduce you, and to talk to him about changing my living situation."

"Us too," Beni piped up, and Juni nodded. The twins had been perched on Neera's lap, watching their arrival with wide-eyed fascination.

"Not me," Udasi snorted. "No time for pompous Kissats."

Tangari laughed. "You wound my pride, old male."

"Eh. You'll do." The Manigan male had been extremely suspicious of Tangari's interest in Neera, but the captain had gradually won him over. It had probably helped that he too was an excellent baduka player. "Still staying here."

"Then the rest of us will go." Arcosta picked up the twins and offered Claire his hand. "Are you ready, kimati?"

"As ready as I'll ever be."

As they descended the landing ramp, the hangar door opened and a new male appeared. He must be Rafalo, Claire decided, as he stalked towards them. He reminded her of an older and much more flamboyant version of Tangari. Neera exclaimed in delight at the sight of him and threw herself into his arms. Claire heard Tangari growl and saw Arcosta put a restraining hand on his arm.

"He is her cousin," he said softly. "Her much older cousin."

"I still don't like it." Tangari started towards the two of them just as an excited shriek came from the entrance to the hangar.

A Kissat female, dressed in multiple layers of floating fabric, came rushing towards Neera. The girl assumed a resigned expression as the female fluttered anxiously around her, exclaiming in distress and acting as if the girl was no older than the twins. Claire could see why Neera might have felt a need to escape.

"Now you're coming home with me right now and will forget that all the silliness ever happened," the mother said as they drew closer.

"No, mother, I'm not. I'm going to travel with Tangari."

From the look on Tangari's face, Neera's announcement was a surprise, but he immediately nodded in agreement.

"What? No, not again!" Neera's mother wailed a protest. "Can't you see that he's no different than that horrible male who took you away from me last time? Rafalo, you have to do something."

"He's very different," Neera said indignantly, while Rafalo studied the captain.

"We will talk," Rafalo said, and Tangari gave a curt nod.

"You don't have to do anything of the kind, Tangari. I'm an adult, and I make my own decisions." Then Neera bit her lip, and turned back to Rafalo. "Although I am very, very grateful to you for sending Arcosta to my rescue."

"Indeed. It appears to have been a very successful mission." The station owner's penetrating gaze traveled from where Arcosta's tail was wrapped around her waist to the twins perched in Arcosta's arms, watching the entire scene with huge dark eyes. "My mate is very fond of children. Perhaps you would care to join her while I discuss business with Arcosta? She is also human," he added.

The elegant female that Neera had described? She drew her cloak more closely around herself, acutely conscious of the wretched hospital gown and the makeshift shoes that Arcosta had made for her, but she nodded. It would be nice to see another human again.

"I will escort you," Arcosta said firmly.

"Why don't we all go?" Rafalo suggested, including Tangari

in his glance. Neera's mother made a muffled protest, but Rafalo simply ignored her. "Follow me."

"Where are we going?" she whispered to Arcosta as Rafalo led them through a series of dark and rather depressing corridors. The thought of living here was growing less appealing by the minute.

"I do not know. I have never been to this part of the station before."

"That is because you were an unmated male," Rafalo said from ahead of them, even though Arcosta had responded just as quietly.

Neera shot her mischievous glance over her shoulder, and Claire remembered what she had said about Kissat hearing.

"Why would that make a difference?" Arcosta asked.

"You'll see."

They went through two locked doors before they finally emerged in a wide white corridor. Small shops and eating establishments lined both sides and she even caught a glimpse of a small park. It was nothing like Arcosta had described, and she gave him a puzzled look.

He shook his head, looking equally confused. "This is very different from the rest of the station."

"It was designed to be." Rafalo waved them along. "Specifically, it was designed to be a refuge for people escaping from desperate situations."

They entered a tiny beautifully landscaped garden just as the doors in a wall at the far end of the garden opened. A stunningly attractive black woman stood there, a welcoming smile on her face. Despite the smile, Claire immediately felt intimidated. Rafalo's mate was as elegant as Neera had indicated, even though she was dressed in nothing more than some simple white pants and a matching tunic.

"Hello, I'm Alicia. I'm Rafalo's mate—for my sins."

The station owner laughed and put his arm around her waist. The obvious affection between them made Claire smile. It was nice to know that she wasn't the only one who had found a mate amongst the stars.

Beni and Juni were still riding in Arcosta's arms, looking around with their wide-eyed gaze, but Juni suddenly wiggled to be let down. Arcosta gave Claire a questioning look, but she nodded. Based on everything she had seen so far, they were amongst friends.

As soon as Arcosta put Juni down, she trotted over to Alicia, staring up at her face.

Ignoring her pristine clothing, the older woman kneeled in front of her.

"Hello, sweetheart. What's your name?"

"Juni," Beni announced. He had followed his sister over. "She doesn't talk. Much," he added.

"Perhaps she doesn't need to," Alicia said calmly, as Lukat poked his head up out of the carrier. "And who's this?"

"That's Lukat. He saved our lives."

"Then he's obviously a very important pet. Would he like a snack? For that matter, are the two of you hungry?"

Beni nodded enthusiastically, and Alicia looked over at Claire.

"I'm sorry, I should have asked first. May they have a snack? Or more if it's time for their meal."

She looked genuinely repentant, and Claire's initial annoyance vanished.

"It was mid-morning on ship time, so a snack would be fine."

"It's mid-afternoon here. I hope you will all join us for dinner."

"I don't want dinner," Neera's mother insisted. "I want to know what you're going to do about that male."

She jabbed a finger in Tangari's direction and both he and Neera stiffened.

"Mother, I told you—"

"Arcosta, Tangari, and I are going to have a talk," Rafalo interrupted smoothly. "Why don't you return home, Murak? I'll come by later."

"Neera, come with me," Murak demanded, then her face crumpled when the girl only looked rebellious. "Please, Neera. I've missed you so much."

Neera's face softened, and she shot a quick glance at Claire. Claire gave her an encouraging smile, and the girl finally nodded at her mother.

"Very well, but I'll return for the evening meal, if that's all right with you, Mistress Alicia," Neera said quickly, before her mother could object.

"Of course."

Neera gave Claire a quick hug, kissed both of the twins, and left with her mother. Alicia smiled at Claire.

"Won't you come inside? We could have some tea while the children eat—or something stronger if you prefer. I have some exceptionally delicious sparkling wine that I've been saving."

"That actually sounds rather tempting," she agreed, then looked up at Arcosta. "Will you be back soon?"

"Of course I will. Be safe, kimati."

An unexpected lump appeared in her throat as she watched them walk away. She suddenly felt as if she was never going to see him again, and she had the strongest urge to run after him and demand he stay. Instead, she forced herself to follow Alicia into her house.

CHAPTER TWENTY

As soon as they were inside, Alicia reached for Claire's cloak. She reluctantly handed it over, and the older woman actually flinched at the sight of the hospital gown.

"Oh my dear. What did they do to you?"

Claire looked down at the twins, and forced a smile. "I haven't had a chance to go shopping."

A hint of dark rose appeared on Alicia's elegant cheekbones. "Of course not. Please forgive my rudeness. This way to the kitchen."

A young Kissat girl was working there, and she smiled shyly as Alicia introduced her.

"This is Yetta. She's an absolute wizard in the kitchen. We've been trying to re-create cookies—do you think the twins would like those?"

She laughed. "I'm quite certain that they would."

Once the children were settled with a plate of cookies and a glass of some type of milk and Lukat was gnawing happily on a small bone, Alicia pulled Claire aside.

"I'm not trying to be rude again, but can I offer you something else to wear? I hope we can shop for the twins later, but there's no need for you to wait until then. I have tons of clothes, and I'm sure I have something that will fit you."

"I..."

"At least come and take a look. We human females have to stick together."

Claire hesitated, then nodded reluctantly. She felt uncomfortable taking charity, but she knew she would have been happy to do the same if their positions were reversed. And she was really, really tired of the horrible gown.

"That would be very nice of you."

The next few minutes disappeared in a world of color and texture. She would probably have been happy with the first thing she tried on, but Alicia had very definite opinions about clothing and, Claire had to admit, an eye for what suited her. She ended up with two gowns and two sets of pants and tunics like the ones Alicia was wearing. Alicia would have given her more, but she put her foot down at that point.

Alicia left her alone to change and she chose a set of pants and matching tunic in a pale blue that made her eyes look almost blue. Her throat threatened to close as she looked at herself in the mirror. She looked almost like the person she had been on Earth, what felt like a lifetime ago. But she was no longer that person and even if she'd had the choice, she would never choose to leave Arcosta and the children. She smiled at her reflection, and went to join Alicia in the main room of the house.

As promised, Alicia opened a bottle of sparkling wine, and Claire took a grateful sip as she looked around. The children and Lukat were playing in the garden outside the wide windows, and there was a reassuring normality to the scene.

A small ping sounded, and Alicia rose gracefully to check a communications device.

"Rafalo wants you to join him. I can take you to one of the doors to the main part of the station, and he'll have a guard waiting there to escort you the rest of the way."

She sighed and rose to her feet. She had just started to enjoy her visit, much more than she had originally expected. Alicia's home felt comfortable, not Earthlike exactly, but with some of that same familiar pleasure. The only thing it was missing was the sky. The view through the windows to the landscaped gardens was undeniably beautiful, but only a cool white ceiling arched over the gardens.

"What about the children?"

"It will only take a few minutes to escort you to the gate. I'll have Yetta keep an eye on them while I'm gone—if that's all right with you?"

She felt surprisingly reluctant to leave them, but they were playing happily, and she was afraid that this was going to be an adult conversation.

"I'm sure that will be fine. You will come right back?" she added anxiously, then blushed. "I'm not trying to tell you what to do, but I worry."

"That's quite all right. After everything you've been through, I wouldn't expect anything less. Do you want to tell them goodbye?"

"Maybe it would be better not to disturb them. I don't want them to worry."

"It's probably for the best," Alicia agreed, leading the way to the front doors. She stopped there long enough to pull out a cloak in the same shade of blue as Claire's new outfit.

"Even though you'll have a guard with you, it's better to be cloaked in the main part of the station."

"Thank you."

She wrapped the pretty new cloak around her, suddenly nostalgic for the cloak that Arcosta had created from the tarp. It was going to be surprisingly difficult to adapt to having real clothes again.

Alicia led her along the market street to a door half concealed behind a large stall. She exchanged greetings with several vendors along the way but didn't stop to chat. As she had promised, it only took a few minutes. After checking a small door panel, she opened the door to reveal a big, grey alien in a dark uniform.

Her skin crawled as he swept his eyes over her cloaked form, but he bowed politely and spoke respectfully to Alicia.

"You are escorting this lady to Rafalo?"

"Yes, Mistress Alicia. He will not keep her for long."

"Very well." Alicia pressed a quick kiss to Claire's cheek. "Don't worry. I'll look after the twins, and when you get back, we'll have a nice dinner. And some more wine."

She forced herself to smile, even though she still hated leaving them. As soon as she stepped through the door and it closed behind them, the guard took her arm.

"That's not necessary."

"It is for your protection. This is a dangerous place."

She nodded reluctantly, even though she hated the feel of his fingers on her arm. And as he hurried her through more dark corridors, she suspected his assessment was correct. The area was sparsely populated, but she had learned enough of the language to recognize the signs indicating bars and gambling houses. The area where Alicia and Rafalo lived seemed much more pleasant in comparison. *Even without the stars,* she thought.

The guard came to a halt in front of a dark, barred door, and she frowned up at him. This didn't seem like the type of office Rafalo would have preferred.

"Is this the right place?"

"Absolutely," he said, grinning.

His smile revealed a disturbing number of sharp teeth, but she did her best to avoid flinching away from him as he opened the door and practically pushed her inside. As the door closed behind her, the lights came on and revealed a rather seedy-looking waiting room with a few bedraggled chairs. *This can't possibly be correct*, she thought, just as a door on the back wall opened.

"You really shouldn't have run from me, Claire," Dr. Pagalan said.

CHAPTER TWENTY-ONE

A rcosta and Tangari followed Rafalo silently into his spacious office. Banks of monitors lined the walls, from which Rafalo could observe everything happening on the station. He waved them over to a comfortable seating area and then joined them, a bottle of old Alluvian brandy in his hand. He poured each of them a drink, and then raised his glass.

"To a successful rescue."

The brandy left behind a soothing warmth as it burned its way down into his stomach, but that only seemed appropriate. Claire and the twins had brought warmth into his own lonely existence.

Rafalo leaned back in his chair, studying Tangari thoughtfully.

"So you and my cousin have developed feelings for each other."

"We have."

"She is very young."

"I'm aware of that. And I'm aware of what happened to her, of how she was betrayed. I am prepared to take my time."

Rafalo laughed. "You're not the one I'm worried about. I don't believe Neera intends to wait."

Tangari took another sip. "What do you suggest? If she does not want to wait, my instinct will always be to do what makes her happy."

"As is true for all mates," Rafalo agreed, then sighed. "I will not insist on a long courtship, but I do request that you give her mother time to become accustomed to the idea. She is a foolish female, but she loves her daughter."

"And if she does not come around? I do not want Neera to think that I don't want her."

Rafalo laughed again. "I don't think that will be a problem. And if Murak is still reluctant, I will speak to her."

"Thank you," Tangari said sincerely.

"Why don't you begin by going to their home? You can introduce yourself more properly to Murak, and then escort Neera to our dinner tonight." Rafalo raised an eyebrow. "I have heard you can be quite charming. Try using some of that charm on Murak. I suspect it will not take long for her to accept you."

Tangari laughed and rose to his feet. "I have to return to my ship first, but I will act upon your instructions as soon as I can."

He swept them both a bow, and left.

"He is a good male," Arcosta said quietly.

"I agree. If I did not, I would never have allowed him into the inner area." Rafalo's voice held a hint of steel, a reminder that he was the powerful male who controlled the station.

"You have managed to keep that secret very well."

"I believed so, although lately, I have heard... not even rumors, really, but whisperings." Rafalo suddenly looked tired. "It can be difficult to balance the two worlds."

"Will you allow me to balance them? To continue my work in the service base and have a home with Claire and the children in the inner area?"

"Is that what you want?"

He hesitated, then shook his head. "Not really, but it seems like the best option until I can rebuild my savings."

"What happened to them?"

"I bought one of the children." He smiled at the quickly hidden shock that crossed Rafalo's face. "It seemed like the best way not only to ensure her safety, but to keep Dr. Pagalan's attention long enough to scope out the security at the lab."

"The lab? My cousin was the victim of a scientist?"

"No, he was just holding her as a favor for the slaver. Claire and the children, they were his victims." He took another sip of his brandy and told Rafalo the whole story.

By the time he finished, Rafalo was scowling at his empty glass. "Every time I think those bastards can't do anything worse, they surprise me. I will do everything I can to put a stop to it."

"Thank you," he said sincerely. If anyone could halt the scientist's work, it would be Rafalo.

"But you are forgetting something," Rafalo continued. "I promise to pay you for this job."

He shrugged uncomfortably. He didn't like the idea of accepting payment, but he couldn't deny that the additional credits would be welcome.

"I was hoping to use those funds to pay for housing in the inner area."

"You would be most welcome to join us, but I may have a better suggestion. Another one of my cousins was involved in a rescue mission last year. Coincidentally, he also worked with a Cire warrior to rescue the female in question. The warrior settled on Alliko—are you familiar with it?"

"Not specifically, no."

"Like all of us, they were affected by the Red Death, but they have rebounded quite well. Their system of government is comprised of a series of city-states, and the Cire of whom I spoke is in charge of one of them—as a legacy for his adopted daughter." Rafalo gave him a meaningful look. "He too is mated to a human female, and I think he would welcome an able mechanic to his territory."

His heart started to beat faster. Was it possible that he could provide Claire and the children with a planetside home?

"I would be very grateful if you could inquire. It might take me a few years to make the payments on a shop, but I will work diligently to pay it off as quickly as possible."

Rafalo laughed again. "My friend, I do not think you understand. You rescued my cousin, a female I love as I would a daughter. Not only that, you saved a human female and two children. I am the one who is in your debt. I am quite sure that there will be something suitable, and it will be my pleasure to give it to you."

"But I cannot—"

"Don't tell me that you cannot accept. I could purchase a hundred mechanic shops for you, and I would still be in your debt." An alarm sounded on the monitor board, and Rafalo looked up and scowled. "Fuck. Another Vedeckian ship has docked. I should have been notified earlier."

"Why do you let them land here?"

"It's part of that balance I mentioned. By not closing my doors, I make it possible to gather information about the slavers and their victims." He sighed. "But I hate it every time one of them comes here."

He frowned up at the screen, and then his face suddenly hardened. He strode over to the desk and slammed his hand on a button.

"Elyat," he barked. "The Vedeckian ship that landed a little while ago. Who is it registered to?"

"Captain Kwan."

Arcosta was on his feet immediately. "That is the one who stole Claire and took her to Dr. Pagalan."

"The one who tried to sell my cousin," Rafalo added grimly. "My desire for information only goes so far. That bastard is going to pay."

"What about Claire and Neera? Are they safe?"

Rafalo nodded as he strapped on a weapons belt, and threw another one to Arcosta. "The inner areas are well protected."

But as he opened the door to the office, a small figure came flying in. Juni threw herself at Arcosta, tears streaming down her little face.

"Mama," she sobbed. "The bad man is here."

CHAPTER TWENTY-TWO

Despair raced through Claire at the sight of the scientist, but she refused to give Dr. Pagalan the satisfaction of admitting her fear. She lifted her chin defiantly as she took a cautious step backwards, fumbling for the door handle behind her back. Her fingers closed over the cool metal, and she tried to open the door. It didn't budge.

Dr. Pagalan tittered. "You didn't think I was going to lose you again so soon, did you? Now come with me. I want to see if that last experiment was a success."

She remained where she was, her back pressed against the wall.

"What last experiment? You said it was a failure."

"Not that one, you stupid female. The one I did the night before you so inconveniently decided to leave. Although I do not entirely blame you." He waved a magnanimous hand. "I'm sure that ridiculous Cire was behind it all. Understandable, I suppose, under the circumstances."

"I have no idea what you're talking about." But despite her denial, her mind was racing. If he had performed another procedure, was there a possibility that she was pregnant after all?

Dr. Pagalan sighed. "I am surrounded by imbeciles. It was quite obvious to me that the Cire had formed a mate bond with you."

"You thought it was obvious then?"

Was it possible? Had Arcosta known from the moment he met her? Even under the circumstances, the knowledge created a little spark of warmth inside her. It also reminded her that he would come for her.

"Of course it was obvious." The scientist sneered at her. "I am trained to observe."

"You didn't observe Arcosta's fist before he knocked you out," she said calmly. "I doubt you'll see it the second time either."

His face darkened as he glared at her. "There won't be a second time. Now come along, I have tests to run before we leave."

Leave? Despite her attempt to remain calm, the knowledge that he intended to remove her from the station horrified her. How would Arcosta find her? For that matter...

"How did you find me?" she demanded.

"It was obvious to a person of any intelligence. I had Captain Kwan trace the purchaser of the Kissat female. He was quite annoyed when he realized that it led back to this station." He tittered again, the unpleasant sound raising the fine hairs on the back of her neck. "I believe Kwan now intends to make the owner pay for that mistake."

"Pay? Pay how?"

If the slaver had a grudge against the station, how far would he go? Her heart started to race even faster. What if Arcosta and the children were in danger?

Her increasing panic must have been obvious because Dr. Pagalan gave a satisfied smile.

"Kwan was grateful enough to bring me with him, and to arrange for my introduction to the male who brought you here. Really, a most useful male, although quite expensive. We will be safe."

"I'm not worried about us," she snapped.

He frowned at her, then shrugged. "Kwan's vengeance is of little concern to me. If you come with me and let me run these tests, I'll tell you what he plans to do."

She didn't trust him, not even an inch, but if she could learn anything about what the Vedeckians had planned, maybe there was some way she would be able to prevent it. She knew it was a long shot at best, but if there was any chance of making sure that Arcosta and the twins didn't come to harm, she didn't have a choice. With a reluctant nod, she forced her fingers to release the doorknob and stepped into the room.

She wanted to slap the look of smug satisfaction off of the scientist's face, but instead, she followed him meekly into the next room.

Despite the terror chilling his blood, Arcosta forced himself to keep his voice low and soothing as he patted Juni's fragile little back.

"Is Dr. Pagalan the bad man?" he asked gently.

She nodded, her breath still coming in shuddering sobs. "He has Mama."

He shot a look at Rafalo over her head, and the station owner nodded grimly. "On it."

The other male returned to his desk, his fingers flying over the controls, as Arcosta concentrated on Juni.

"What about Beni? Is he all right?"

She nodded firmly, and he breathed a sigh of relief.

A stream of profanity erupted from behind the desk, and he looked over as Rafalo slammed his hand down on the surface.

"Alicia received a call from someone supposedly speaking on my behalf. They knew your mate was there, and they knew about the inner section of the station." He started swearing again, and Arcosta covered Juni's ears. "I suspected there might be an issue, but I had no idea it had gone this far."

"I also do not think it is a coincidence that the Vedeckians showed up now," Arcosta added grimly.

"I agree. And although I had every intention of confronting them directly, I am not sure that would be the wisest choice." Rafalo punched several of the controls on his desk, then nodded. "They're locked in the hangar. It will require my personal code to override the lock."

Juni patted his chest urgently, her sobs finally dying down to a few hiccups. "Mama."

"We are looking for her, little one," he promised, giving Rafalo a worried look as the other male continued to scan for any sign of Claire. His body quivered with the need for action, but it was a big station and he knew it would be foolish not to wait until he had some idea.

She patted his chest again. "I know."

"You know where she is?"

She nodded urgently, her silky pink locks flying. He didn't hesitate, but started for the door.

"How could she possibly know?" Rafalo called after him. "You should wait until we find her on the scan."

"If she says she knows, she knows." He had no idea how, but he trusted his daughter.

"I'll keep monitoring and send help if you find her," Rafalo promised, his voice fading as Arcosta took off at a run.

Juni directed him through the market—this one offering

little more than bars and gambling establishments, the smell of pasha smoke heavy in the air—and despite his anxiety to find Claire, he shuddered at the thought of his tiny daughter making a way through here to find him. They quickly turned into a more deserted section, down one narrow corridor after another until she tugged him to a halt, placing her small hand over his mouth as she pointed to the next corner.

Moving silently, he peeked around the corner. A big Orsonian stood guard outside the heavy door, and his heart sank. He had no doubt he could overcome the Orsonian in combat, but he didn't know if he could reach him in time to prevent him from raising an alarm. Unfortunately, he didn't see any other alternative. He placed Juni gently on the ground.

"Wait here, little one."

She shook her head and grabbed his arm.

"It is too dangerous for you. You have to wait."

She shook her head, and for the first time a tiny smile crossed her face.

"Wait," she whispered, pointing at the corner again.

The need for action was beating at him, but he obeyed and took another look. At first, he didn't see anything different, just the unfortunately alert guard, but then he caught a flash of pink. Lukat appeared at the other end of the corridor, scampering merrily towards the guard. The male turned to watch him, staring at the small animal. He raised his staff as Lukat approached, but before Arcosta could intervene, Lukat made a seemingly impossible leap and landed on the guard's shoulder.

The male let out a shriek as the gosa sank his sharp little teeth into the vulnerable area. He swung wildly, trying to dislodge Lukat as the gosa bit him again, and then Arcosta reached them. Carefully avoiding Lukat, he broke the guard's neck with one swift twist. Lukat jumped on his shoulder as the guard collapsed, chittering happily.

Juni trotted up, seemingly unperturbed by the body on the floor, and pointed at the door. He tried it, but as he had expected, it was locked. A quick search of the guard's body revealed the keys, and he silently inserted one into the lock, turning it carefully. The door opened into a small dirty waiting room. An empty waiting room.

He bit back his disappointment and headed for the door on the far side of the office. The second room was obviously an exam room, bare and clinical. It too was empty, but he caught a hint of Claire's sweet scent lingering in the air, along with a terrifying trace of blood.

By Granthar, if Dr. Pagalan was trying to use Claire as the subject of another one of his twisted experiments, he would feed him to the station disposal.

Yet another door led out of the exam room, but he hesitated, looking down at Juni. She had picked up Lukat and was holding him close.

"It might be best if you stay here, little one. I'll lock the door so no one can get in."

He hated to leave her, but he wasn't sure how much further he would have to chase Dr. Pagalan and Claire and, given the smell of blood, what condition she might be in when he found her. With the doors locked, at least Juni would be safe.

She immediately shook her head, and he wished he knew if it was simply a child's determination not to be left behind, or if she knew she would play a part in what was to come.

"I know you want to find your mama, but I can track her from here. Are you sure you wouldn't rather wait here so I know you will be safe?"

She hesitated for a second, a faraway look on her face, and gave a reluctant nod.

"Good girl."

He quickly locked the doors leading to the outer room, then made sure the inner door would lock behind him.

"I will be back as soon as possible," he promised, as he bent down to kiss her goodbye. "I am sure that Lukat will protect you while I'm gone."

She gave a tiny giggle, then nodded and stepped back. The last thing he saw as he closed the door behind him was her small body braced against the wall, her big dark eyes following him.

CHAPTER TWENTY-THREE

"No one can possibly deny my genius now," Dr. Pagalan told Claire triumphantly, as he looked up from his test results.

She refused to give him the satisfaction of a response, her arms crossed her stomach. He had taken more blood from her abdomen, but he had used a different type of needle that had been unusually painful. God, she didn't want to go back to this —to this life of experiments and pain and disappointment.

Please hurry, Arcosta, she prayed silently.

Dr. Pagalan scowled at her lack of response. "You are no longer interested in my results? I was under the impression that you wanted to become pregnant."

Pregnant? The world swirled around her, and she had to clutch the exam table to keep herself from falling.

"I thought it wasn't possible."

"Perhaps not for a lesser male, but I am a genius."

With his wild-eyed glee, he never looked less like one. *More like Dr. Frankenstein,* she thought bitterly, and swayed again. He had said she was pregnant, but how—and with what?

"How?" she whispered, her voice shaking.

"Now you're interested?" He smirked at her, and she wanted to scream in frustration. But he was too proud of himself to remain quiet for long.

"That wretched Cire turned out to be useful after all," he said smugly.

This time, her knees did give out, and she collapsed down to the ground. *Arcosta?* Arcosta had been part of Dr. Pagalan's experiments? The pain of that betrayal far eclipsed the pain of the needle, but then she shook her head.

"I don't believe you. He would never do anything like that."

"Perhaps not consciously, but fortunately, he wasn't intelligent enough to realize what was occurring when I took the sample from him." Pagalan shook his head in mock sadness. "I do hope the children turn out to be more intelligent."

The shocks just kept coming.

"*Children?*"

"Of course. Even you must have realized that I have been working on producing twins. You are carrying two embryos."

In spite of everything, her heart gave a little leap of joy. Twins, just like Beni and Juni. Or...

"Do you mean that Arcosta is the father?"

"Didn't I just say that? Really, I am beginning to despair of these children having any intelligence whatsoever. I will have to test them thoroughly once they are born."

The conflicting rushes of joy and terror switched back and forth so quickly that she felt dizzy, but she did her best to force them under control. There was no way she was ever allowing Dr. Pagalan to get his hands on her children. She knew Arcosta would come from her. She just had to figure out a way to delay the scientist until he did. But even as she thought that, Dr. Pagalan ordered her to her feet.

"Come along now. I don't want to be here when the Vedeckians create their little surprise."

"I'm not going with you."

He tittered. "You have no choice in the matter."

She folded her arms over her chest and glared at him. With an aggrieved sigh, he bent down and grabbed her arm. Since she'd been wearing the shock collar when she arrived, he'd never had to physically force her to do anything. She had somehow assumed that his stocky little body was as weak as it looked. Instead, he hauled her to her feet with surprising strength.

"If you do not start obeying me, I will take those children from you," he hissed.

Her arms automatically tightened across her stomach. "You can't do that. You need them to show your experiment worked."

"The embryos will prove it." He shrugged. "It might even be possible to grow them in an artificial environment. I would prefer to allow the experiment to proceed naturally, but if you don't cooperate, I am quite prepared to find an alternative. Now, through that door."

She obeyed. He might be making an empty threat, but she couldn't take the chance.

Please, Arcosta, she thought again as she tried to come up with a way to leave a trail. *Hurry.*

ARCOSTA FOUND A NETWORK OF CORRIDORS ON THE OTHER side of the exam room. One set led back towards the more populated area of the station, but the trace of Claire's scent went in the other direction. He frowned as he started to follow it through a maze of utility corridors. Why would Dr. Pagalan be taking Claire into this section?

At least there were no other scents interfering with hers

and he could easily follow her tracks. He was sure that he was gaining on them when the trail came to an abrupt end at a blank wall. *No!* He couldn't lose her. He knew he had been following them up until now. Unless...

What if they had doubled back? In that case, it might be possible that he had missed something. Just as he was about to try retracing his steps, he saw a tiny spot of blue at the base of the wall. When he bent down to examine it, he found that it was actually lodged in a small gap. The corridor didn't end here —there was a concealed door.

It took far longer than he would have liked to find the hidden catch that opened the door, but at last it slid silently to one side.

Behind the door was a huge, cavernous space lined with machinery and crisscrossed by a network of catwalks. He realized that they had reached the center of the station, containing the machines used to run the station. The space was dimly lit, the only light provided by the control panels on the front of many of the machines, but he could see Dr. Pagalan and Claire were halfway across the space. She was alive and, as far as he could tell from here, unharmed. A vast sense of relief rushed over him even as he hurried after them.

With the deafening noise of the machinery, he wasn't concerned that they would hear him coming. He forced himself to keep a steady pace, rather than an outright run, concerned that the vibration of the catwalk would alert Dr. Pagalan. Unless they looked back, he should be able to take the scientist by surprise. Even as he thought that, Claire gave a quick, desperate look over her shoulder. Hope washed across her face, but she had the sense not to react. She resolutely turned her face back in the direction they were headed.

He was still several steps behind them when she stumbled. Dr. Pagalan swore, audible even over the other noise, as he seized her arm. Unfortunately, as he did so he saw Arcosta approaching. He immediately pushed Claire against the narrow railing that was the only thing separating her body from the emptiness below.

"Stop right there or she goes over."

Anger and fear threatened to choke him, but he obeyed.

"Good boy," Dr. Pagalan's voice oozed satisfaction. "This is what is going to happen. You are going to turn around and go back to the far side of the cavern. You will remain there while we leave because if you take even one step in this direction, I will push her over."

"He won't," Claire said desperately. "He needs me to prove his theory worked."

Arcosta growled as he saw the scientist's fingers digging into Claire's arm.

"There are other females."

"But they're hard to get. And think how long it took for it to work with me."

Dr. Pagalan's experiment on his mate had been successful? What had he done to her?

"I would prefer not to start over, but I will if necessary."

"If you harm one hair on her head, you will not be starting anything again. You will be dead," he said coldly. "I am not going anywhere."

For the first time, Dr. Pagalan actually looked shaken. He looked at Arcosta, then at Claire, then at the remaining distance to the exit door.

"You cannot out run me." His tail lashed eagerly.

With a frustrated snarl, Dr. Pagalan suddenly thrust Claire towards Arcosta, then turned and ran for the exit. Arcosta hated to let him go, but it was far more important to catch Claire as she stumbled forward. Before he could reach her, there was a deafening roar, and then the whole space shook. He heard Dr. Pagalan scream, and caught a glimpse of the scientist falling over the low railing, but all his attention was focused on Claire.

He watched in slow-motion horror as the catwalk swayed and her body tipped slowly and inevitably towards the emptiness below. He lunged for her with every ounce of speed and strength that he possessed. Her fingers brushed against his, but he couldn't grasp them. Her face was white with terror as she started to fall over the railing, and then his tail closed around her wrist, holding her in place as he pulled her back onto the catwalk. He collapsed down on the still shaking metal, his arms and tail wrapped around her as he shuddered.

"I knew you'd come. I knew it," she whispered over and over again while she clung to him just as desperately.

"I have never been so scared, kimati."

"Neither have I. I knew you'd find me, but I didn't know how long it was going to take." She took a long shuddering breath. "How did you find me so quickly?"

"Our daughter, of course. She came to find me."

"By herself?"

"She brought Lukat—who proved to be a great warrior. But we need to return to her as soon as everything stops shaking."

Claire looked around at the still quivering catwalks and the machine flashing red alarms. "What happened?"

"I have no idea."

"Dr. Pagalan said something about the Vedeckians seeking revenge. I wonder if this is what he meant."

"Captain Kwan's ship had just docked," he said grimly. "It is possible. I hope there is not too much damage."

Her face went pale again. "What if Beni was hurt? Or Neera?"

"Look around," he said soothingly. "The machinery is still running, despite the alarms. We have oxygen and gravity. And

Rafalo already had the Vedeckian ship locked down. I suspect any damage will be external."

"But Tangari's ship was in one of the docks—and Udasi!"

If Udasi had been hurt after he had been the one to encourage him to leave Maniga, he would never forgive himself.

"It's possible that Tangari's ship might have been damaged," he admitted reluctantly. "But it's more likely that it was nowhere near the blast. For that matter, we don't even know that there was a blast."

The catwalk finally stopped shaking, and he helped Claire to stand.

"Let us go retrieve our daughter and check on everyone."

An odd look crossed her face.

"What is it?"

"I have something to tell you, but I'd rather wait until we know everyone is safe and we're alone."

"Did that bastard do something to you?"

"I'm fine," she said soothingly, if vaguely. "Please, can we make sure everyone is safe first?"

"Very well," he agreed reluctantly, determined to do so as quickly as possible.

CHAPTER TWENTY-FOUR

Claire paced nervously back and forth as she waited for Arcosta to return. As they had speculated, the Vedeckian ship had exploded. There had been extensive damage, but because the ship had been locked in the dock, the only fatalities appeared to be the Vedeckians themselves. Apparently, they had intended to leave the bomb behind and detonate it from a distance, but because of the lockdown, they had been unable to leave. They still weren't sure why it had detonated anyway.

The communication system had also been damaged as a result of the blast, and they had been relying on written messages. Because of the extent of the damage, Arcosta had reluctantly left her and the children with Alicia and gone to join Rafalo in the search and rescue efforts. In addition to checking for anyone who had been wounded, they were also verifying that the hull of the station was intact.

Thankfully, no one in their own little family had been hurt.

They had returned to the exam room to find Juni waiting for them, her face calm as she stroked Lukat's fur. She had thrown herself happily into Claire's arms, and she had been the one to pat Claire's face soothingly when she cried.

Arcosta had gathered them all up in his arms, then set off for the inner section as quickly as he could. There had been little damage there, nothing worse than a minor earthquake, but Beni and Alicia were anxiously awaiting them.

"I am so sorry," Alicia apologized again and again. "I don't know how she got away from me. Beni said she was fine, and Rafalo said she was with Arcosta, but I've been so worried."

The older woman burst into tears, and Claire hugged her.

"Everything turned out fine. If it hadn't been for her, I'm not sure that Arcosta would've found me in time."

She shuddered as she remembered tipping over the railing, certain that she was going to fall to her death. If Arcosta hadn't been there, she was sure that she would have died along with Dr. Pagalan.

Alicia gave her a watery smile. "I'm sorry. I'm not usually this emotional, but losing track of Juni, and not knowing what was happening after the explosion when I couldn't reach Rafalo... It's been a difficult day."

"I agree." She hesitated. "Under the circumstances, I hate to even ask, but I really need to talk to Arcosta alone. Do you think you could watch the twins again? Just for a short time?"

"You would trust me to do that?"

"Of course. Juni is... special. She knew what needed to be done, and I don't think you could have stopped her."

"I'm still not going to let her out of my sight this time," Alicia promised.

Neera had been fine as well, although distraught with worry about Tangari. She had been fighting with her mother about going to look for him when they returned. She had reluctantly agreed to stay behind with Claire while Arcosta went to check on Tangari and Udasi.

Before he could leave, Tangari came rushing in, equally concerned about Neera. Ignoring everyone else, he pulled her into his arms and kissed her frantically. Claire saw Neera's mother's face when he did, and she thought that Murak accepted the inevitable at that moment.

Udasi had stubbornly remained on Tangari's ship, dismissing the whole thing with a wave of his hand. Tangari told them that he'd said it was nowhere near as bad as the "real storms" on Maniga.

Now the communication system had been restored, and Arcosta had sent word that he would be returning soon. They were all spending the night with Rafalo and Alicia, and Alicia had suggested that Claire talk to Arcosta in the room she had given them.

"I've always found difficult discussions work best in the bedroom," Alicia said, her eyes twinkling.

"I don't think this will be a difficult discussion," she had told Alicia, but now that she was waiting for Arcosta, she wasn't quite sure.

He had already proven with the twins that he was a wonderful father, and she was sure that he would love their children. Eventually. But she couldn't help wondering if he would be upset about the method, or worse, suspicious as to what Dr. Pagalan had actually done.

Knowing that she was getting worked up, she took a deep breath and wandered over to the long open windows. Outside was a small courtyard with boulders covered in rich purple moss artistically arranged around a small stream. Other than the unusual colors, it reminded her of a Japanese garden, and she tried to use the serenity of the space to calm her nerves. She thought she had succeeded, but she practically jumped out of her skin when she heard the door open behind her.

She whirled around to find Arcosta standing there. He

looked tired, and for a moment she almost reconsidered, but then his gaze traveled over her and his eyes heated. He didn't look tired anymore.

"You are a very welcome sight, kimati. And while I had no complaints about your previous attire, I do find this outfit very appealing."

Her cheeks heated, but she smiled as she walked towards him, the silky fabric swishing around her legs. The long deep blue dress reminded her more of a nightgown than an actual dress, but Alicia had assured her that it was quite acceptable for eveningwear. The neckline dipped a little lower between her breasts than she would normally have chosen, but given the way Arcosta was focused on that slice of exposed skin, she couldn't really object. Her nipples tightened under the intensity of his gaze, and she had a momentary impulse to put off the conversation and lure him into bed instead.

No, she decided reluctantly. *That wouldn't be fair. He needs to know.*

Apparently he hadn't forgotten the earlier conversation either because even though his tail curled around her waist and he pulled her against him, he didn't kiss her immediately.

"What is it you wish to speak to me about, kimati?"

"Dr. Pagalan told me that his last experiment was a success," she blurted out.

"What experiment? Did he hurt you?"

"Not really." His face hardened at her choice of words, and she hurried on. "He said that when you were at the lab, he took a sample from you. Do you remember that? Do you know what he was talking about?"

"He did not do anything of the—" He stopped and tilted his head thoughtfully. "When we had tea, he scratched me with his ring. I did not think anything about it at the time, but he would have had a sample of my blood as a result. Why?"

She focused on his shirt, nervously plucking at the fastening, rather than looking at his face.

"He said he already knew that you thought I was your mate."

A gentle finger lifted her chin so that she was looking up at him once more.

"He was correct. I think I knew the second I saw you, but as soon as my tail touched you, I was positive."

"He said that's why it was possible."

"Why *what* was possible? You are being very evasive, kimati." Amusement and frustration vied for dominance on his face.

"He said that I'm pregnant. By you. With twins."

For the second time since they met, he staggered, and once again she pushed him gently down onto the bed.

"Pregnant?" he whispered. "With my child—my children?"

"He seemed very certain. I know it's not the most conventional way to get pregnant," she hurried on. "But you don't mind, do you?"

"Mind?"

He yanked her down on top of him and kissed her until she was writhing helplessly in his arms, then suddenly pulled back, looking appalled.

"I did not think. Was I too rough? Did I hurt the babies?"

She laughed, giddy with happiness.

"You have never been too rough with me. And considering the babies probably aren't even as big as my fingernail yet, there's no way you could have hurt them. You're going to want to wrap me in a protective bubble the entire time I'm pregnant, aren't you?"

"I will take the utmost care with you."

"You know that pregnant females have a lot of aches and pains," she said thoughtfully.

His expression immediately turned worried. "I do not wish you to be uncomfortable. What can I do? Would you like me to rub your legs?"

"I'm sure that will be very nice. In the future. Right now, I have a different kind of ache. Here." She cupped her breast. "And here." Her fingers trailed down between her legs.

His eyes gleamed black. "I would be happy to take care of those for you. Is it safe?"

"Not only safe, but necessary," she assured him as his mouth closed over her nipple, hot and wet through the thin cloth, and his tail slid under her dress to seek the needy ache between her thighs.

He lifted his head long enough to give her a solemn look.

"I will devote myself to making sure that every ache receives my attention. I love you, Claire."

Tears sprang to her eyes, and she wondered if it was too early to blame them on her pregnancy.

"I love you too, Arcosta."

EPILOGUE

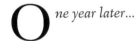O*ne year later...*

CLAIRE SIGHED AS SHE WALKED INTO THE NURSERY AND saw the empty crib. She returned to the living room to grab the box of sweets that Udasi had sent, then smiled and added a blanket and a bottle of wine before she went to find her mate. He was exactly where she expected him to be, in the big swinging couch on their roof deck. The twins were asleep on his chest as he rocked slowly and looked up at the stars. Their skin was a paler green than his, but other than that, they looked just like him. The only part of her they had inherited was their grey eyes.

"I suppose they couldn't sleep again?" she asked dryly.

He gave her an innocent look.

"They were restless."

"At some point, you're going to have to let them sleep in

their crib." Just like Beni and Juni had done, the twins slept curled together in a single bed.

"But they are so small."

"Small and perfect," she agreed as she nestled against his side.

A perfect little girl and a perfect little boy, just as Dr. Pagalan had predicted. As always, she had conflicting feelings when she thought of him. He had been callous and cruel—and quite probably pathological—but he had been responsible for their beautiful children.

Arcosta's tail wrapped around her waist and pulled her closer. She took a deep breath of his spicy scent and let Dr. Pagalan return to the past where he belonged.

"Are you finished working for tonight, kimati?"

"Yes." She smiled up at him. "The numbers look good."

"Rafalo will be pleased to hear that."

With the station owner's backing, she had been creating a small loan program for the town. It was a far cry from the multi-million-dollar deals she used to arrange, but it was far more satisfying. Udasi's new bakery had been one of the first loans they had approved, and he was already halfway to paying it off. The only downside was that because the twins—both sets— kept her so busy during the day, she ended up working at night while Arcosta took over child duty.

"I had a call from Tangari today," Arcosta said thoughtfully.

"How is he? How's Neera?"

The month-long courtship that Rafalo had originally insisted on had lasted less than two weeks before the couple were mated—with the full approval of Neera's mother. Neera had been accompanying Tangari on his ship ever since.

"Homesick, apparently." He shook his head. "She did not find traveling as exciting as she thought it would be."

"Oh, dear. And you said he loves it."

"Not as much as he loves her." He hesitated. "He is flying in next week so we can talk about it some more, but he is interested in purchasing a share in the shop. What do you think?"

"I would love to have them close by, and you know the kids would love it too. But are you okay with the idea?" She knew how much having his own business meant to him.

Everything about the home Rafalo had found for them on Alliko had worked out—this house on the edge of town with its view of the stars and the nearby mechanic's shop with a steady stream of business. Craxan, the Cire warrior managing the territory for his adopted daughter, had welcomed them with open arms, and his human mate Joanna had become one of Claire's closest friends. Even their children got along well together, although Beni might have been a little too smitten with Tavi, Joanna's daughter.

They're just children, she reminded herself.

"I think it would be perfect," Arcosta said easily. "It would free up some of my time so I can be here more during the day. So I can spend time with my beautiful mate."

"And your beautiful children," she added dryly as she caught the sound of footsteps flying up the stairs.

"Mama, Mama! Is it true?" Beni burst onto the rooftop in a ball of energy. He never seemed to stop moving these days, but it was such a welcome change from those silent days in the lab that she never attempted to slow him down.

"Is what true, sweetheart?"

"Juni says Auntie Neera and Uncle Tangari are coming to live with us!"

Beni climbed up on the swing with an energetic bounce. Claire smiled at Arcosta over his head as Juni came to join them too, Lukat frolicking around her heels.

"It's not definite yet," Arcosta warned, but Juni smiled knowingly as she climbed up next to her.

Claire had no idea how her daughter knew these things, but she undoubtedly had a gift.

"They can have my room," Beni said magnanimously, and Claire had to hide her grin. They had only recently tried separating the older twins, but most nights they still ended up together.

"They might want their own house," she said gently.

"Are you going to build it, Papa? Can I help?"

Without waiting for a response, their son launched into a list of all the items he considered essential in a new home. Arcosta listened attentively while Claire cuddled Juni and looked up at the stars.

"Now it's time to go back to bed," she announced when Beni finally wound down. "The babies too," she added pointedly.

After everyone was settled, she took Arcosta's hand and led him back up to the roof.

"I thought you said it was time for bed," he teased.

"Our bed tends to become the family gathering spot. I want some time alone with my mate first. Why don't you open that bottle of wine?"

She spread out the blanket as he did, then waited until he turned towards her. As soon as he did, she let the gown slip down to the ground. She was wearing nothing beneath it.

Arcosta's breath caught at the sight of his mate, naked in the moonlight. She seemed to grow more beautiful every day.

"Are you in need of my attention, kimati?"

"Yes. I ache here."

She stroked a finger down her neck, and he obligingly bent his head to nibble gently on the spot she loved. She shivered happily, and he saw her nipples grow dark and swollen.

"What about here?" he asked, circling the taut little buds.

"Definitely."

He lifted her high into his arms so that her breasts were in front of his mouth and he could lavish his attention on first one, then the other. He could feel her sweet cunt growing slick and hot against his chest and slipped his tail between their bodies to tease her pleasure pearl.

"Have I ever mentioned that I love your tail?" she gasped.

"Frequently. Perhaps more often than you tell me you love me."

Her body stilled, and she reached down to put her hands on his cheeks. "That's impossible. I love you most of all."

"I know, kimati. Just as I love you." He lowered her down far enough so that he could kiss her breathless. When he finally raised his head, he grinned at her. "But that does not mean we cannot have our favorite parts. And right now, I think my favorite is your hot little cunt."

He lowered her onto his aching cock as she laughed and moaned simultaneously. Even after all this time, he still had to work his way inside her, the tight grasp an exquisite torture. They both sighed once he was fully embedded, then he slowly started to lift her free. He could feel her quivering and knew that it wouldn't be long before she climaxed. Since he suspected he would follow her, he carefully lowered them, still joined, to the blanket.

He lifted her over him, her beautiful body silhouetted against the stars as she began to rock slowly back and forth. In spite of the urgency he could feel building in his spine, he let her take her time, let her choose when to increase the pace until finally she was clinging to him urgently, gasping his name. He grabbed her hips and brought her down hard over his cock, once, twice, three times until she threw back her head and shuddered, her cunt pulsing around him and triggering his own climax as his knot expanded and locked them together.

She fell forward onto his chest and he wrapped his arms around her, stroking her hair as she slowly relaxed. He knew the second she fell asleep in his arms, but he was content just to hold her as he looked up at the stars. He had his house and his land, he had the stars, but most importantly, he had his mate and his children. He had found his home.

AUTHORS' NOTE

Thank you for reading *A Home for the Alien Warrior!*

We truly enjoyed writing Claire and Arcosta's story. Although our hero and heroine had a whirlwind romance - filled with daring escapes and delicious interludes, we also loved writing those moments where they truly connected as partners and parents.

Plus, it was a joy to have Claire and Arcosta embrace those who needed a family, such as the adorable and resourceful Juni and Beni, the grumpy-but-kind Udasi, and the adventurous Aunt Neera and Uncle Tangari. Lastly, bringing Rafalo and Alicia into any *Treasured by the Alien* story is always an absolute pleasure!

Here we are, six books later, yet this series would not be possible without the following people...

To Our Fantastic Readers: Thank you for your love and support of this series. We are incredibly grateful that you enjoy tales of loving, alien warriors who finally find their treasured, human mates as much as we do!

To Our Awesome Beta Readers, Janet S., Nancy V., and Kitty S.: You've helped us tell wonderful stories. Thank you so much for your time and feedback. We treasure you so much!

To Our Fabulous Cover Designers, Naomi Lucas and Cameron Kamenicky: Every-dang-time you guys nail it! Juni and Beni are exactly how we envisioned them. They are beyond cute as they're held in their father's arms. Perfection!

To Our Loving Families: Your love and support mean everything to us. (Seriously. All that cooking and cleaning wouldn't have gotten done by themselves.) Thank you for all you do. You're the best!

Again, we are so grateful that you've read our book! It would mean the world to us if you left an honest review at Amazon. Reviews help other readers find books to enjoy, which helps the authors as well!

All the best,
Honey & Bex

The *Treasured by the Alien* series will return in 2022! In the meantime, you can enjoy another found family in Honey's next book, ***A Gift for Nicholas*** - a sweet and steamy holiday tale!

Can a single mother show an arrogant alien warrior the true meaning of the holidays?

A Gift for Nicholas is available on Amazon!

If you would like to be kept up to date on all the latest news—including release dates—please visit our websites and sign up for our newsletters!

www.honeyphillips.com
www.bexmclynn.com

OTHER TITLES

Treasured by the Alien
with Bex McLynn
Mama and the Alien Warrior
A Son for the Alien Warrior
Daughter of the Alien Warrior
A Family for the Alien Warrior
The Nanny and the Alien Warrior
A Home for the Alien Warrior

Cosmic Fairy Tales
The Ugly Dukeling by Bex McLynn
Jackie and the Giant by Honey Phillips

BOOKS BY HONEY PHILLIPS

The Alien Abduction Series
Anna and the Alien
Beth and the Barbarian
Cam and the Conqueror
Deb and the Demon
Ella and the Emperor
Faith and the Fighter
Greta and the Gargoyle

Hanna and the Hitman

Izzie and the Icebeast

Joan and the Juggernaut

Kate and the Kraken

Lily and the Lion

Mary and the Minotaur

Nancy and the Naga

The Alien Invasion Series

Alien Selection

Alien Conquest

Alien Prisoner

Alien Breeder

Alien Alliance

Alien Hope

Exposed to the Elements

The Naked Alien

The Bare Essentials

A Nude Attitude

The Buff Beast

The Strip Down

Cyborgs on Mars

High Plains Cyborg

The Good, the Bad, and the Cyborg

A Fistful of Cyborg

A Few Cyborgs More

The Magnificent Cyborg

The Outlaw Cyborg

Horned Holidays

Krampus and the Crone

A Gift for Nicholas

Anthologies

Alien Embrace anthology

Pets in Space 6 anthology

Claimed Among the Stars anthology

BOOKS BY BEX MCLYNN

Standalone Books

Rein: A Tidefall Novel

The Ladyships Series

Sarda

Thanemonger

Bane

Printed in Great Britain
by Amazon

76406303R00123